12 NIGHTS

12 NIGHTS

AYLA COX

12 NIGHTS

Copyright © 2024 Ayla Cox

To reach Ayla, feel free to email her at:
AylaCoxWrites@gmail.com.

CONTENTS

DEDICATION

Some of us like it a little merry and bright...

*But this one is for those of us that want to feel
the blood of the guilty coating our fingers.*

CONTENT WARNING

Please be cautious of your mental health as you enter this book.

- Intense and Dark Sexual Themes
- Violence and Murder: Graphic depictions of violence, including acts of retribution and killings as part of vigilante justice.
- Abuse and Torture: Descriptions of physical and psychological torture, including mutilation.
- Sexual Assault/Abuse: Mentions of sexual violence and rape, with themes of retribution against perpetrators.
- Manipulation and Deception: References to con artistry, emotional manipulation, and betrayal.
- Trauma and PTSD: Characters dealing with emotional and psychological scars from their past, including flashbacks and the aftermath of violence.

- Moral Ambiguity and Justice: Themes around vigilante justice, blurred lines between right and wrong, and the emotional conflict of acting outside the law.
- Addiction and Substance Abuse: Mentions of drug use as a form of control and coercion.
- Guilt and Internal Conflict: Characters struggling with feelings of guilt, shame, and fear about their actions and decisions.

1

October-November 2022

The grift was a simple one I normally could've run with my eyes closed. I'd researched Lord Azreal King, a timid and private businessman, for weeks. It was difficult to find much of anything. He was born in Winchester to a Sudanese mother and a British father. When his father died a decade ago, he inherited a fuck ton of money from the estate. By all accounts, he was a single loner who kept to himself: he was the perfect mark.

Lord Azreal oversaw a security consultant agency that I couldn't find much information on. That itself was my sign to be careful. My prep had to be immaculate because if he found out who I was, he could make me disappear without a trace.

When the day came, I was ready. But I was also fucking freezing. Everyone says that your blood thickens up after a few years, but I was still the same popsicle I'd been since I moved to the UK four years ago with Auntie June. We'd run so many cons together in the past seven years, but I missed running them alone.

I only needed four weeks to gain access to his mansion. Jordan would take his grandfather's centuries-old jewelry collection and disappear like mist on a hot day. With priceless artifacts on my mind, I mentally prepared myself for the con. I waited as Jordan, standing out of sight near the lunch spot he frequented by the London Westfield.

When Lord Azreal breezed out of the door with some tall man with an angular face, I only had eyes for him. They shook hands and the other man walked in my direction. At just the right time, I walked into Az's path.

It looked like I was so caught up in my phone and the Louis Vuitton and Burberry bags that I'd accidentally dropped my wallet. I kept walking, waiting with bated breath for him to notice. I made it five steps before he called out to me.

"Miss!" The deep bass ran right up my spine and caught me off guard. I wasn't expecting it.

Turning, I gave him my best puzzled look. That's when my jaw dropped. The two pictures I found of him didn't do him justice. But, I don't think anything could've prepared me for the pure magnetism exuding from his brown sugar skin. Azreal was breathtaking. The cream turtleneck hugged him and provided the perfect contrast with his glowing hue. The way his peacoat hung from his shoulders, it was clearly crafted for him.

I guess that's when it started. When I saw him, it felt like I'd stuck my hand inside a light socket and the electricity was flowing between us. He was perfect—and that was something I hadn't prepped for. It threw me off my game.

My skin heated in a blush as his eyes moved up and down for a cursory glance before he handed me my wallet. As I reached for it, my fingertips grazed his wrist, and his brown eyes widened as his pupils dilated. We were silent as I waited. He was supposed to make the first move. I'd carefully crafted my outfit to include twelve different conversation starters. Instead of looking for an in, he nodded and turned to leave without saying another word.

That's when I panicked and asked, "Can't I at least say thank you?"

Except it was in the wrong accent. Jordan was French-Canadian—not American.

He turned, this time he gave me more than a cursory glance. This one was a slow drag that made me feel like he was stripping me down, right there on the sidewalk. The intensity in his eyes was gone a second later as he flashed me a polite smile.

"It's alright," he said. His eyes dropped to my bags and back before he cocked his head to the side. "Los Angeles?" he asked.

Kicking myself, I didn't answer his question. I flashed him a smile of my own and hoped my blush looked like a reaction to the cold. I held out my hand.

"Jordan Lewis," I said, sticking with my own accent. There was no going back now.

He brought my hand to his lips, grazing my knuckles with a kiss. "Azreal King."

Heat began to fill my cheeks again as his thumb brushed across my fingers, and I wanted to melt on the spot. His skin was so smooth.

"Are you on vacation?" he asked, maintaining eye contact.

I had to remind myself to breathe, "I'm here for work," I said.

My head was fuzzy because his thumb was continuing its work across my skin. Using my accent had fucked it all up. I needed to regroup and rethink how I could make Jordan American, but he was throwing me for a loop.

"Do you have plans tonight, Jordan Lewis?" The way he said the name went right to the apex of my thighs.

"Are you asking me out, Azreal King?" My voice was breathy and his gaze fell to my mouth.

"Say yes," he said, his smile widening.

Three hours later we were sitting in the back of a hidden speakeasy in Earl's Court. When Azreal suggested it, I was surprised. I didn't expect a speakeasy to be his vibe, but I was grateful I didn't have to press for something off the beaten path. The chance of someone recognizing me was higher than I liked. There weren't many size sixteen black women wandering around expensive restaurants.

When Azreal showed up, he was just as stunning in the dim lighting as he'd been in the sunshine. He flashed me a smile and greeted me with a soft kiss on the cheek that made my insides dance in anticipation. I blinked against the unfamiliar feeling and gave him a smile of my own.

"Jordan. What are you drinking?" he asked, sliding into the booth beside me instead of in front of me. His hand raised, and he made eye contact with the waiter.

"Cider is fine for me," I said, trying not to seem too knowledgeable. Playing American was fine, but I still needed to seem like a fish out of water. I couldn't start off the date telling him that if the waiter gave me a cider that tasted like candy, I would throw it at them.

When the waiter made his way, he looked between us.

"Hey mate, what cider do you have on tap?" Az asked. The waiter rattled off a few brands, and I bit my cheek. Azreal picked something strong and slightly sweet, and I smiled at him as the waiter walked away.

Once the drinks arrived, I immediately took a pull right from the cider bottle, ignoring the offered glass. Azreal sipped at his bourbon and laughed a little to himself.

"What?" I brought my hand to my face, thinking I'd splashed myself.

"I didn't think a woman wearing boots worth a thousand pounds would drink right from the bottle."

I laughed from my belly, before taking another sip. "What can I say? I'm an enigma."

He watched me as he took another drink, his eyes doing another slow crawl of my exposed skin.

"Don't tell me you have hidden piercings and tattoos."

"Nah. I wish," I replied, turning a little more toward him and his outstretched hand behind me.

"Well, what tattoo would you get?" he asked as his fingers, traced a small circle against my upper arm.

"You're sure you want to ask me this?" I eyed him, trying to see if he was serious. When he nodded, I cleared my throat. "Sekhmet. She's powerful and capable of war and destruction, but that's not all she is. People depict her as bloodthirsty, but she is as much a healer as a destroyer. If I get a tattoo, that's the first thing I'm going for."

Azreal stared at me, something far away in his gaze. He licked his lips and squeezed the skin of my arm, sending a shiver up my spine. I grabbed my bottle by the neck and took a long pull, relishing in the burn going down my throat and trying not to think about this man's closeness.

"What would you get? Or do you already have one?" I wiggled my eyebrows and took him in.

"I've never really thought about it," he replied, distracted.

"I'm going to ask you again in an hour. I hope you have a better answer. Okay, new topic. Are you as obsessed with Christmas as I am? Or are you the embodiment of Scrooge?"

He startled before letting out a guffaw so loud that a few different tables turned to look at us. I barely noticed them because of the way he lit up when he laughed. The laughter reflected in his eyes, and the surrounding lines deepened. And there was even a little, tiny dimple that appeared on his left cheek. I was going to have to keep making this man laugh. It looked like he needed it.

That night we stayed up for hours drinking and talking. When the night was over, he called me a ride and opened the door, whispering good night. When he kissed both my cheeks, he lingered, filling my senses with the smell of whiskey and leather. I closed my eyes so I could soak it in—soak him in.

When the car started moving, I felt my phone vibrate in my purse. I turned to see Azreal holding his phone to his face, and I picked up mine.

"I just pulled aw—"

"Meet me next Saturday for dinner. A proper dinner."

I fiddled with the edge of my coat as I looked out the window. "Of course."

It wasn't until I got home that I realized I wasn't acting like Jordan at all. I was acting like Eden. And I was playing a dangerous game by revealing so much of myself to my mark. But, for some reason, that game was more thrilling than it should've been.

Every weekend after that, we went out.

He told me about how hard it was growing up split between two cultures while walking through the British Museum. I told him about how I was waiting for the right thing to keep me centered while drinking coffee from Pret A Manger and staring at the Thames.

I told myself I needed that invitation to his Winchester mansion those first few dates. And his grandfather's collection would be mine, and I'd be gone. But I didn't push. Hell, I didn't even make a move to kiss the man. I was almost scared to. It was as if the connection between us was strung too tight, and neither of us wanted to take a chance on it evaporating.

We were on our sixth date in four weeks when he pulled something from his coat and handed it to me. He smiled at my shocked face and watched as I tore through the plain wrapping.

"Happy Christmas," he said as I revealed the gift.

It was a book about *Ma'at*. Sekhmet was on the cover, her face a mask of severity and her lion's mane flowing behind her, a scepter in her hand. My mouth fell open as I touched the cover. He'd remembered.

That's when I leaned forward and reached out my hand to touch his lips. I felt their soft heat beneath my fingers, and he softly inhaled as I gently felt them. When he grabbed my hand, I leaned forward and captured his mouth.

The kiss was chaste, but the way that my stomach hippity-skipped made it the best kiss I'd had—ever. As I pulled back and looked at him, a small sliver of worry distracted me from his soft smile. Somehow he reached past my meticulous planning and kept pulling the truth from me. Our connection was profound. No, it was more than that—it was real.

Jordan—no, *I* was fucked.

2

December 24th, 2022

Falling in love was supposed to be invigorating. The dim world was supposed to be filled with light while everything became new, fresh, and phenomenal. But all I felt was anxious.

I'd never really been in love before, but that was by design. My life wasn't built for love. Love was the opposite of what I needed to do the job. But I was fucked because Jordan *was* in love.

I knew it the second that present came out of Azreal's coat pocket. And I'd been trying to come to terms with that fact for days. The book was a fascinating deep dive into all nine layers of existing in harmony. My captivation with Egypt started with my mom, and when she passed away, it was the one thing that made me feel close to her.

Az didn't know that, but he cared anyway. And that was dangerous as hell. Love or not, I needed to complete this con. I couldn't risk him learning who I was and this feeling that I had swirling around in my chest made me want to come clean, and that was unacceptable.

That's why I went to Winchester. I told myself to get what I needed that night because this needed to end. It wasn't that I was unable to keep the lies straight anymore, it was because they were no longer lies. The only lie I'd ever told him was that my name was Jordan. And his knowing so many truths about me put my real identity in danger.

The plan was a simple one: tell him I'd been fired, cry a little bit, and when he put me in a room and left me alone to gather myself, I would go right to where I knew the heirlooms would be based on the blueprints.

Clearing my throat, I pulled out my cell phone to call him from the back of the cab. I cracked my neck to relax into Jordan. It was important to get the tone right. He needed to be so worried about me that he wasn't concerned about me invading a space he hadn't invited me into. The call almost went to voicemail, but he answered just in time.

"Hello," he answered, his tone surprised.

"Azreal," I said, sniffing.

"Jordan, what's wrong?" he replied. His voice was so full of concern that my stomach lurched. The refrain popped into my head again. *It's not his shit, it belonged to his fucked up family.*

"I– are you in Winchester?" I knew he was. He'd told me he would be home on Christmas Eve, but this was the moment of truth. It wasn't clear if he felt the same way that I did. But this. This moment would be telling. If I hadn't built trust with him, he'd lie, and I'd be fucked.

"I am. Are you okay?" his tone was becoming more urgent, and the guilt went from a lurching to gnawing.

"Can I," I let my voice hitch, "can I come by? I just don't know where else to go." I closed my eyes, trying to fight the nausea creeping up my throat.

"Of course. Where are you?"

"I'm in a cab."

He rattled off his address and I repeated it, knowing that my driver was already on his way to the correct address.

"Can you stay on the phone with me?" I asked, my eyes misting at the care that was in his voice.

"Of course. Of course," he whispered.

The sound of his breath on the other line both calmed me and filled me with dread. The push and pull got worse the further we drove out of the city and towards his country home. It had been in his family for hundreds of years, and when we got closer, I saw all the things you'd expect an old manor to have. The large, ominous hedge maze towered taller than it needed to. The house finally came into view, and it all became real.

"I'm here," I breathed into the phone.

When I saw him standing at the front door, barefoot, with a look of worry on his face, the plan was ruined. The car hadn't even come to a full stop before I was out the door and eating up the distance between us. All I wanted to do was run my hands across his body and his skin. And that's precisely what I did.

When I found myself within reach, I grabbed the front of his shirt and pulled his mouth to mine. I felt the electric pulse of our connection against our lips, and I devoured him. He gasped against me as his hands caught me around the waist. I moaned, feeling the fire in my soul grow so hot that I felt like I was going to explode.

The door slamming shut echoed through the entryway, but I barely heard it. My focus was on the way that my body was combusting from the inside out as he held me against the front door and pulled off my jacket.

His hand found my breast through my shirt and his touch was light. I moaned when his thumb brushed against my nipple. The touch became a pinch, and I wanted to melt into the ground. I lifted his shirt that he'd neatly tucked into his jeans to feel his bare skin, almost coming on the spot.

As my hands undid his jeans, Az pulled his mouth away from mine and I found his waist with my thigh.

"Jordan?" he asked against my lips. "What do you need?"

"You," I replied. He caught my eyes, and his hand found my cheek.

"You have me."

His fingers pulled aside my panties under my dress, finding me soaked. I freed his dick from his jeans and he was sinking slowly into me, his mouth attached to my neck as he held my hips in a bruising grip.

"Fuck," he called out against my skin.

"Please," I moaned, my pussy so soaked I could feel the wet gathering between my thighs. His tongue traced my skin as he pushed forward, stretching me. I groaned as I felt his balls slap against me, and he held himself still.

I rocked against him, my hips rolling as I slipped effortlessly back and forth on his length. The moan he let out went straight to my clit. His fingers tightened on me, and he pulled my skin into his mouth. I angled my hips as he slid just a little bit deeper, and I felt him shudder. He kissed at the skin he'd been biting and sucking as he held my hips still.

"Jo—"

"Make me cum," I said, cutting him off. If he called me Jordan one more time, I was sure I would burst into tears. I could see the question in his eyes, and I pulled his hand from my hip and touched the inside of my arm, tracing the plastic. "Birth control."

His eyes widened as he traced the small rod, moving from my arm, past my breast, to my waist. He didn't stop his trek until his fingers met the space where we were merged. Wet digits swirled against the mess I was making, finding my clit and moving against it. My eyes closed as the pleasure buzzed through me.

"Look at me," he moaned as his pace increased. I brought my gaze to him, and his lips sipped at mine as my orgasm bared down on him. That's when he started moving his hips, fucking me through my gasps and moans.

His thrusts were rhythmic. Each stroke stoked an inferno in my belly, making me ravenous for everything he had. I wanted to fall into him as he slowed his pace.

"Don't. S-st-stop," I moaned, my eyes still on his.

What little control he had seemed to break, and his easy thrusts became erratic. Sweat sheened his face, and I leaned forward, licking a drop from his skin. The sound that came from his mouth was guttural as his fingers left my pussy and grabbed my waist as he pulled all the way out and slammed back into me. My grunt spurred him on. Three more thrusts and he was coating my pussy in cum.

He leaned against me, his breathing erratic as he caressed my skin. My fingers found my pussy and I swiped at his thick cum, popping a digit into my mouth and humming.

"I've got something for your mouth. Come." His hand grabbed my wrist, and I trailed after him, leaving my panties by the front door.

There was plenty for my mouth and a lot more coming before I fell asleep, thoroughly spent, in Az's arms.

I was alone when I woke up. It was silly to think that I'd finally get a glimpse of the parts of him that he seemed to keep behind a wall. But the way he'd held me and caressed my skin as we laid in stunned silence; there was something between us that neither of us wanted to speak to. But I knew I would never forgive myself if I let this secret continue to fester between us. What we'd shared had changed our relationship forever, and it would be cruel to continue like this—for both of us.

Instead of going to the anteroom that was attached to the library, I went searching for him. He wasn't on the third floor or the second. My socked feet moved slowly down the stairs as I listened for him. The hallway towards what I knew was a wine cellar was lit up. When I entered the room, wine lined the walls, but there was also a door open on the far side.

That hadn't been on the plans.

I moved towards it as I heard muffled crying. It was a whole separate section of rooms. It looked like a prison.

But what caught my attention was the man dangling in the middle. He was shirtless and pale and, from the ruddiness in his face, he'd been upside-down for a while. His mouth was covered in layers of thick tape and the dirt on his skin matched the stink of BO, piss, and shit that wafted through the door.

My whole body felt cold as I watched the scene. I didn't move, I barely breathed. What the actual fuck was going on? I couldn't see much from my vantage point, so I eased closer for a better look. The floor in the room was smooth stone, but the grate directly beneath the hanging man and the supplies organized on the table told me two things: there were his last moments and he wouldn't be the first.

"Are you ready for your judgment?" It was the voice that had just spent hours whispering to me as he filled me over and over. I brought my trembling hand to my mouth. I couldn't see his face, but it was Azreal. In his palm, a large, curved knife flipped as he walked toward the man.

The prisoner was crying and wiggling, but he didn't have the strength to break the binds that kept his hands behind him. His gaze found mine, and he called out from behind the tape as he looked at me, begging and pleading for help. Before I could even process the scene, the knife in Azreal's hand swung up, carving a deep wound into the man's abdomen.

When he pulled the knife free, the sound of blood and whatever else plopped heavily against the ground. My stomach revolted, and my hand tightened on my mouth. The man's screams became shrill as they echoed around the room. He writhed against his bonds, making the blood shower down his chest and across his face faster.

The man's screams didn't stop as the knife dived deep again, this time slicing down into his flesh and exposing fascia and muscle. The heavy sounds of blood pouring only added to the cacophony of the gruesome scene.

Pulling the curved knife, he dug until he could grab a line of intestine and pull it free. The man's teary eyes lost contact with me as he looked toward his executioner. Their blue irises were heavy with fear—and resignation.

Az looked wild. His face and his hands were covered in blood. He began yanking the man's intestines down and around his neck.

That's when I ran.

Azreal was a killer. A brutal murderer who was strangling a man with his own intestines. I'd gone from never being in love to falling for a psychopath. And I'd been lying to the man for almost two months.... What would he do to me once he found out?

My feet took me to where I'd dropped my bag. I slipped on my shoes and I looked towards the stark and empty hallway, practically hyperventilating. When I didn't hear or see him coming, I made my way to the library and pushed open the back door to reveal the artifacts I'd been looking for. I grabbed everything I could and swept it into my handbag.

A set of keys sat by the door and I grabbed them, running towards the garage. The emblem on the key ring was some brand I'd never seen, but it was clear that the car at the end of the garage was the one that the keys belonged to.

Jogging over, I looked behind me one last time as I jumped behind the wheel. Not only was the wheel on a side I'd never driven on, it was a manual. I tried three times to start the car, pumping against the clutch and failing. On the fourth try, I found the right combination, and the car started. The garage button was on the dash and I pushed it as I shifted noisily into sixth gear and peeled off.

Away from the man that I loved but didn't know—and away from my fascination with the gruesome punishment he'd bestowed.

Christmas day was far more cheery at the airport than I expected. I certainly wasn't in the mood to celebrate, but I was ready to leave this country in my rearview. All the airport attendants wore festive headbands and had blinking lights around their necks, and all I had with me was my bag and the clothes on my back.

What was in the bag was more than enough to set me up for a better life once I'd made my way back home to America so I could become Eden again. I pulled up to Southampton airport and bought the first available ticket. I was going to Amsterdam, and I'd find my way back to the States from there. It didn't matter where the flight went, as long as it wasn't here.

But for some stupid reason, I couldn't stop the tears that welled up. Rubbing at my stinging nose, I tilted my head back. No crying. I dug around in my bag, finding the hidden pocket for my passport and the emergency postcard I kept there. My aunt and I had a system in place. If we ever needed to run, we'd drop our card in the post box and wait for the other to reach out. When I handed over my passport, I asked the woman at the desk where I could mail my card, and she took it for me, promising to get it to where it was going.

Maybe she was taking pity on me as she scanned my details into the system. I can imagine how I looked. I'd just been so thoroughly fucked, I could still feel my muscles relaxing and contracting. I was also wearing nothing beneath my dress and didn't have on a winter coat. With that and the murder, I was probably giving crazy eyes.

Standing near my gate, I closed my eyes and replayed that moment. The fear was startling. But, even though, I was traumatized by the look in his eye, something was fascinating about the way his skin gave way beneath the pressure of the blade. And how the bright crimson of his blood trailed down his pale skin.

My fingers worried the edge of the clasp on my bag as I breathed through the emotions I'd felt. Love, lust, pleasure, pain, surprise, horror, terror... But the one that was front and center was hurt. I'd opened myself up, and

I shouldn't have. He was a mark. He wasn't meant to be anything more than that. And yet, I fell in love like an idiot. And then I walked in on a scene right out of a Robert Rodriguez film.

I blinked against the memories and the tears. Rubbing them into my shoulder, I focused on the bustle around me and tried to quiet the voice in the back of my mind. It was telling me to go back, that he could explain. That was the crazy part—I knew that he could.

Some part of me knew Azreal would never murder a man for no reason. And I knew if I saw him, if he touched me, and he looked deep into my soul with those honey-colored eyes, I'd fall right back into him and lose every piece of sanity I had left. It was one thing to finesse people out of their wallets and heirlooms, but murder?

And me, what would he do with me? I'd wormed my way into his life, into his bed, so that I could rob him. He wouldn't care that I'd fallen in love with him. If he knew the truth, I'd be swinging from my ankles next. And, just because I'd briefly considered a tummy tuck in the past didn't mean I wanted to end up with my intestines and other organs outside my body.

The flight doors opened, and I took a shuddering inhale, only for my senses to get clouded by the familiar musky and spicy scent of expensive, one-of-a-kind cologne. His cologne. Doing my best not to fold on the spot and put my arms around him, I shut my eyes and took a breath through my mouth to try and clear his scent from my head.

Even being this close to him made my heart stutter and ache as it beat hard in my chest. Fingers trailed up the bare skin of my arm, every inch of skin he touched ate at my resolve. He knew what he was doing. It was intentional. Specifically chosen to make me remember how easy it was to fall into him, to trust him, to love him.

His forearm gently snaked around my waist, pulling me back into his warmth. As he held me, everything around us melted away. I couldn't stop myself from covering his arms with mine and taking in the softness of his skin and the way my body reacted to him being so close to me. My nipples got stiff, my pussy slick, my mouth salivating at the idea of tasting him again. Keeping my eyes shut did nothing to stop the images of us together from playing like a movie behind my eyelids.

A wave of emotion clogged my throat as I whispered, "Az." Tears cloyed on my eyelashes as I held on to the sob, threatening what little control I had left.

His hand came to my chin, pulling me close enough that I could feel the stubble of his 5'o'clock shadow, and his lips came to the tear that broke free from my eyes. The stuttering sound I made led him to pull me closer to him as he kissed my other cheek and rested his forehead against mine before burying his face in my neck.

"Jordan," he said, into my skin.

It was the reminder that I needed that I wasn't innocent in this, either. He was a killer, but I was a liar and a thief. Jordan, with all her secrets, all her baggage, had gone and fallen in love with Az and I couldn't be Jordan anymore.

I didn't need to open my eyes to know that his eyebrows were drawn tight; that his stubble made him look more handsome than unkempt; and, even in this abrasive light, his deep skin was practically glowing. It was how he'd always looked.

"Azreal, let me go. Please." My voice shook, but I meant the words. I didn't think I could say them, not to his face. But like this, my eyes shut tight in a crowd of hundreds. I could say the thing that made my heart feel like it was being torn straight from my chest.

Time stretched between us, him holding me, his lips drifting into my hair as he audibly smelled the scent of me the same way I found myself breathing in the scent of him. I'd said the words I needed to, but I held on to him as much as he held on to me.

But then his arms retreated, and I felt the chill seeping all the way through me, and it shattered my heart. Something was placed in my hand, and I pulled it close to my chest as my tears began to fall freely.

"You'll need me. And I'll be waiting for the day that you do," I heard him say behind me. His absence was so heavy that I didn't even need to turn to know that he was gone, even though his scent lingered around me. The gate agent called for the last to board, and I had to force my feet to move. I didn't want to—I wanted to stay. But staying wouldn't fix what I'd done.

I walked to my gate and handed them my boarding pass from my pocket. He'd given me a cell phone with a long antenna tucked into the side. It was a satellite phone. One that, he'd no doubt programmed with his number. I hoped I'd never need it, but my heart hurt so much that there was no way I was going to throw it away. I tucked it into my bag. And walked through the gate.

I didn't look back.

3

I'd been stealing since I was twelve years old. A psychologist might connect it to losing my mom and getting sent to a group home, but I think it was the only thing that made me feel like I hadn't died too. It was small stuff here and there until I got caught. The social worker was asking me all kinds of questions and, baby, the show I put on for that lady should've won me an Academy Award because I got away with a slap on the wrist.

When I realized I could act the part and get what I wanted, it was nothing but up from there. When Auntie June found me, I was twenty-two years old and standing outside the Ritz in New York City holding a brand-new Chanel that some idiot's credit card had paid for. My hand was up, hailing a cab, when she looked me up and down.

All I heard her say was, "That was a nice pull," and I booked it. It took six months for her to convince me that she wasn't a cop or looking to be my competition. She saw something of herself in me, and she wanted to see what I could do up close. In reality, she was tired of grifting alone and wanted a protégé. She taught me everything from skimming credit cards to building personas and planning escape routes.

But I'd fucked up.

The last thing I said to her was a hastily written, *Sorry, xxx* written on a postcard I couldn't even be sure she'd gotten. When I got the call from a solicitor saying she'd passed, I was shocked. It had been almost two years since I'd sent my postcard and every month I checked my empty PO box, hoping she'd sent one, that she'd come looking for me. But she never did. And now she never would.

Part of me held out hope that it was a ruse. That June was fine, and it was all a reason to get me on a flight back to Britain. But I'd seen her. Her face was still and perfect in repose. She was gone. She was gone, and I'd fucked it all up. Hopefully, she understood now why I had to run.

Why I couldn't say goodbye, and why I wasn't here for her in her final days.

Aunt June had demanded a quick funeral, and that meant two days after the call, I was here in the city I swore I wouldn't ever set foot in again. I'd barely made it in time for the funeral. But I couldn't risk it. As much as I wanted to speak to her, to apologize, I was stuck in the shadows, watching from a distance.

After the funeral, I just wandered, trying to breathe in the city and quiet the guilt that was heavy on my heart. The Christmas decorations were just as intense in Camden as I'd remembered. It was good to see that some things didn't change. Decorating for the holidays started painfully early here, and I always hated it. Decorating the day after Halloween should've been criminal, but since they didn't have Thanksgiving as a buffer, Christmas was pretty much two months long.

In an ideal world, I would've taken my time, reacquainting myself with the city that used to be my home. Visiting my local to see if Duffy was still tending the bar. Walking every single floor of the Tate to see the paintings I'd spent hours studying. But this wasn't the ideal visit or the ideal circumstance. There was an invisible noose around my neck, and if I wasn't careful, it was going to tighten, and I'd lose what little I'd built for myself since I'd left.

I had one stop to make before I headed back towards the airport to hop on the first flight back to New Mexico. There was something of my mother's in my old storage unit. I'd paid ahead, far ahead, so it would be a quick in and out.

That's why it was so unfortunate that I didn't catch the rustling behind me as I entered the corridor near my garage. I heard a gun cocking as the icy cold metal pressed against my neck. It wasn't a surprise, not really. It was bound to happen. The second I hopped on that flight, I knew there would be demons to face and fear to conquer. But this demon? This one wasn't even on my radar. His reflection was distorted in the glass beside me, but I'd know that Quasimodo face anywhere—Harden Driscoll.

See, I'd taken him for a little bit of a ride, both figuratively and literally. I knew he'd been looking for me, but I didn't think he'd still be this desperate a decade later. Yeah, I was memorable, but this seemed excessive. I could understand if I'd taken millions from him, but at most, I'd only managed to get away with fifteen thousand pounds...

He was one of the first hard lessons I learned when I moved to London. Some of these rat bastards were cash-poor and pretending to be rich. I almost laughed at the irony of it being him. June watched me work him for six months, knowing he was broke as shit. She'd bought me a drink once I realized what a massive waste of time it was.

"Sometimes that's how you learn. Don't give me that sad puppy stare, drink your whiskey," she'd ordered as she got me well and pissed before spending the next few days talking through all the signs I missed along the way. And I never made that mistake again.

It should've been an easy choice to stay in America, it's not like Auntie would know—she was dead, after all. But, attending her homegoing felt like it was the least I could do. Auntie was the last person I had left on this earth, and I owed it to her to say goodbye this time.

"Driscoll," I said, not hiding my real accent. He'd known me as a Kiwi named Jessa. That should've been his first clue. A black chick from New Zealand named Jessa? He was just as dumb as I was.

He started speaking, and it sounded like a speech he'd been rehearsing since I'd conned him. "First, love, you're going to empty all of your accounts and give me back what you stole, plus interest. Second, you'll give me back my mother's engagement ring. And third, you're going to suck the skin from my cock the way you used to. Then, maybe I'll decide if I'm ready to blow your pretty fucking brains out." Harden's thick northern brogue was heavier in his rage, and I didn't need to see him to know his pale face was beet red.

"I don't suppose you'll settle for a shandy and a curry? I was hoping to grab—"

A heavy blow came to the back of my head. I stumbled against the metal door, throwing out my hands to steady myself and keep my feet through the pain. I damn sure wasn't going to die on my knees. Blinking through the frustration, rage expanded in my chest as I fisted my hands. Sure, I was pissed at Harden, but mostly I was mad at myself. How had he found me? One of my oldest marks. An easy one. I was slipping.

"Un-fucking-real. How did you get a gun?" I asked, resisting the urge to grab the back of my head and check for blood.

"Turn around," he hissed, ignoring me.

I faced him. He looked high. Shit. He was strung out, his pupils small and his hair greasy and sweaty. I rattled through my options, scanning the hallway and him. The place was deserted, and it was too late at night to hope someone would show up in the nick of time. I watched the sweat beading on his lip as he held the weapon straight. Someone had taught the fool how to use the pistol. The safety was off, and his large finger was tight on the trigger. There was no doubt he'd get a shot off before I could drop-kick his ass.

"Let's go," he ordered, gesturing toward the other end of the hallway. I wasn't going with him. So, there were only two options: die or pull the card liable to destroy everything. Slowly, I stepped forward and watched him take a measured step back.

"No," I said.

"What are you on about?" he asked, confused.

"I'm going to reach into my bag, pull out my phone, and dial a number. If you still want to kill me after you talk to him, feel free." And I did just that. He sputtered, but I kept moving my hand slowly, pulling out the phone I'd kept with me for years. I pressed two buttons and I dialed the only number programmed into it. The line rang once before it was answered.

"It's me," I said, before handing it to Harden.

"Who the fuck is this?" He paused for a few seconds and his eyes went wide. "What?" he asked. His finger left the trigger, and he itched at his head with the barrel. "A million pounds," he hissed angrily, but then his eyebrows shot up, and his arm relaxed at his side. "A. Million?" His mouth fell open for a moment before he mumbled, "Harden Driscoll."

He placed the gun in his hoodie pouch and retrieved his own phone from his pocket. Two taps on the screen, and he laughed, deep from his belly, before doing a little twirl and throwing my phone back at me. Without a word, he turned and walked away.

I watched him go in stunned silence. Threats I expected. Maybe even a little fear. But jubilation? I stared at the phone in my hand and looked around me, half-expecting someone to pop out of a dark corner.

The phone was still connected. I looked down at it, wanting to throw it. I'd used it as a comfort blanket for almost two years, and now it felt hot in my hand. It went black for a moment before it began to vibrate with an incoming call.

I watched it light up with the unsaved number and stared. I was given a chance that Pandora never was: I was able to close the box. But, now, that box was wide open and the contents would never fit back inside—and all the darkness and sin were spewing out.

When it vibrated for the fifth time, I answered. Neither of us spoke, but I could hear the wind behind him.

"Be here in an hour," he said, sounding exactly like I'd remembered, all silk and bass. The line disconnected, and I let my hand fall from my face.

Numbly, I walked outside and let the stinging air hit me. Shaking hands grabbed the hat off my head and I felt the lump starting to form. I'd had worse. He hit like a bitch.

London brought out the best and the worst in me. It was the place where I'd felt alive for the first time, and it would be the place that swallowed me whole. I exhaled, my breath clouding in front of my face, and I watched it lift and scatter away above me. Cheerful lights flickered around me, and I felt my insides lurch back and forth with a cold dread.

Merry fucking Christmas.

After getting myself together, I went back to my storage unit and retrieved the pouch I'd been looking for. Next, I pulled up a map on my cell and tried to find the best path out of the city. Things had changed a lot since the last time I'd been there. When I looked up the TFL map, I confirmed that I could hop on the DLR and get where I needed to go.

An hour wasn't nearly enough time to get out of the city, but with any luck, the airport's security would keep things from getting out of hand. The last time I'd seen Az he was turning intestines into a noose. It turns out, everything I'd stolen was worth almost a million dollars. Something told me that would probably get me fitted with a bowel necklace too. London was a maze of CCTV, it was impossible to move through the city without being tracked. I was fucked if he had access.

But I had to try.

The second I pulled that phone out of my bag, I knew it was over, and it was only a matter of time before I fell into the depths of Az again. In the last two years, he'd become my very own Candyman. I was terrified of him and of what he represented. But at night, when my fingers found their way between my thick thighs, he was the one that I was thinking about. And the thought that I was near him, that he was chasing me, made my pulse race and had me feeling certifiable.

I gave myself a brief moment along the Thames, listening as the water rushed by. The unique briny scent of it filled my nose as the mist floated around, almost hugging my skin. It was half twelve and the area was almost deserted. The park was cold, but London was always cold this time of night. The way that the wind whipped off the water was making me shiver. At least, that's what I told myself was the reason I was shaking. It wasn't fear or trepidation. And it most certainly wasn't excitement.

It wasn't.

It was so odd how familiar everything felt here. Now, standing in front of the river I'd spent so much time watching, I could finally admit how much I'd missed it. It made me think of a time in life when I was different— when my life was different.

I took a look around the gardens, not at all surprised that no one was out. It was a Wednesday night and most of the folks who could afford to live in this area had work early in the morning. With a final glance, I turned and walked toward the Canary Wharf station.

Something gripped my arm and yanked me to the side. My back met someone's front, and I smacked at the body behind me. I was thrashing against the stranger as the anxious beating of my heart tripled. That's when I recognized the scent clouding me. I started to hyperventilate as something sticky was placed against my skin.

"Welcome home, Eden."

The fear of hearing my real name was brief. A dizzy exhaustion flooded me. I didn't even have the opportunity to react as I succumbed to darkness.

4

December 13th, 2024

In the movies, people had the pleasure of waking up disoriented, enjoying a few blissful seconds of hope that everything was fine before being smacked in the face with reality. I wish... I knew exactly where I was, and I should've expected it.

I was back in Winchester Manor.

Controlling me in the city would've been difficult, but his estate? It was miles in every direction before you ran into anyone who didn't get paid not to ask questions.

Everything was still dark, which meant it was probably early morning. I eased off the bed and crept across the carpeted floor. It was cold as fuck. I was glad that I still had my coat and shoes, even if my cell was missing from the pocket. Checking the door, I was surprised that the knob turned. The door squeaked as I cracked it open, just enough for my abundant ass and titties to slide through. I looked up and down the hall to orient myself.

He'd left me on the ground floor of the manor, and I knew exactly where I was. The lit sconces and exposed stone made that clear. Unlike the more characteristic floors above, the first floor was the least decorated of them all. I walked left. I still had dreams about what existed to the right, and I didn't need a reminder of the hidden prison attached to the wine cellar.

As I moved through the manor, I didn't come upon anyone. It felt too easy. Still, I kept each step light as I walked as quietly as I could down the hall. My heart was beating against my rib cage as I saw the massive, decorated tree in the entryway. There were so many presents underneath that they'd probably need their own house soon. The last time I'd been here, the place wasn't nearly this decorated. When I looked towards the door, I saw an electronic lock affixed to it. A shotgun rested on hooks against the wall.

Taking a chance, I tried to open the door, but the latch wouldn't catch. A red light blazed on the left hinge, and I realized I needed a key card to get out. I moved towards the garage and saw that the door was the same. Locked. Walking back to the hall, I looked around for any possible way out and I didn't find one. I could go back to my room and wait, or—I pulled the shotgun off the wall—I could go get that key.

Sconces gave the manor a small amount of light. It was just enough to be able to see the stairs as I took them one by one. The second floor was lavender. All the sconces a deep and vibrant eggplant. But this wasn't the floor he lived on. I crept slower up the next set of stairs and hugged the wall as much as I could, raising the shotgun to my shoulder.

The third-floor sconces were jet black, and so were the chandeliers dangling from the ceiling. The tips glimmered in gold. Blood-red drapes covered the stone walls. I passed one door and then the other, taking a breath as I approached the last door in the middle of the hallway. It was ajar and didn't make any noise as I pushed it open.

As I neared the bed, I couldn't help but remember the sweaty night I'd spent in this room with him. It was something that lived rent-free in my head for years, and now I was seeing him again, in the flesh. I stood over his sleeping form, and I couldn't help but think back to when it was all simple and easy—before I knew the truth about him.

I held the shotgun on him, looking around, trying to spot anything that could've been a key. All I could think of was making my escape, and I couldn't do that without the keys. This was probably my only chance.

As I looked around the dimly lit room, I couldn't help but feel everything I'd tried to seal away since I'd run. The way his eyes would watch me as I walked across a room. His hands, warm against my skin, as he lifted my shirt from my belly. The scent of hawthorn and vanilla clouding my senses while his tongue traced agonizing circles around every inch of my neck.

"Shoot," the deep timbre of his voice moved around me, sweet and sticky like molasses.

My hands were steady, and I didn't budge an inch when he spoke. Instead of retreating, I took three steps closer. I pressed my thumb against the safety and watched the smile grow wider on his face as it clicked off.

The last two years had been kind to him. His bare face now bore a short beard, hiding the dimple that I loved. His cheeks had grown more pronounced and his buzzed head was now a sharp fade with kinky ringlets colliding against one another. Even though his eyes were still closed, every inch of his body was alert.

If he heard the snick of the safety, he didn't show it. His hands were still right where they'd been above the covers, his bare chest visible beneath the pooled sheets. I knew better than to get too close to him, so I kept space between us as I held up the shotgun.

"Let me out."

My demand was met with a throaty chuckle, one that was so charged, involuntarily, I took a step back. He didn't seem at all afraid that I might pull the trigger, but I was.

"No." There was no venom in his tone, only arrogant defiance.

The gun was steady in my hands as I aimed it at his bare chest. Az's eyes opened, gifting me with a scalding look that had only been living in my dreams. He sat up, slow and deliberate, like a hunter tracking its prey. The blankets pooled lower as his palms met the bed and pushed up.

What little change I'd seen in his face was replaced by bulging biceps and a thick core. The tent in the sheets was unmistakable. I put my finger on the trigger.

"Don't tempt me, my lord," I mocked.

"One year, three hundred and fifty-three days," he murmured, ignoring my words and the gun pointed at his bare chest, as he kept his blistering eye contact with me.

"You drugged me," I said, feeling the slither of rage coiling in my belly.

"The patch is perfectly safe," his accent, was still enough to make me want to melt into a puddle.

"Where's the—"

He threw his sheet off, revealing his thick erection. The momentary distraction allowed him to grab the shotgun and angle it up. My finger depressed the trigger and I heard the sound of buckshot hitting and bouncing off the stone walls, breaking glass in the already freezing room as I wrestled with Az and lost just as quickly.

I hissed from the chill of his cold hand on my throat. Snatching the shotgun away from me, he threw it across the room. It skittered and fear filled my gut, stirring with the lust already building. He pulled me forward, achingly slow, his eyes incandescent in the darkness.

"Eden."

"You. Drugged. Me." I hissed, refusing to acknowledge the way my body perked up at the sound of my name—my real name—on his lips.

"You stole from me," he countered, tilting his head to look down past the inches that separated us. Cold air whipped through the room, but all I could feel was the heat from his body flush with mine and the strength of his hand, possessively tight around my throat. My chest heaved as I pulled at his wrist, only to be yanked forward to collide with his lips.

Everything in the room shifted as exhilaration and lust shot through me. His lips were soft and warm as he leaned forward and bit down on my bottom lip before thrusting his tongue forward to tangle with mine. Every swish and flick was aggressive and familiar, and I found myself meeting each stroke with the eagerness of an addict.

He started walking me backward, his tongue continuing its pillage as he moved his thumb across my skin, tilting my face so he could dive deeper into my mouth. His tongue was practically counting each of my teeth and, like the glutton I was, I moaned in delight.

Nothing from before mattered because he was everything I needed. I was finally free to let myself feel the things I'd tried and failed to forget. With my back against the wall, I grabbed at his waist as his dick rested against my abdomen. Sighing, I trailed my hands across his skin, moving toward his length.

Az caught my hand, pinning it up above my head. He brought my other wrist up to meet it. A shiver rippled through my body as I rolled into his. I heard two clicks above me before I felt the weight of something against my wrists, tightening. I yanked at my arms, finding them secured to a metal pole at the top of the wall.

"What the..." I screamed.

He stepped back a half second before I kicked out at him. Metal and leather were secured around my wrists and fastened to o-rings. Even if I was able to contort my fingers back, the keyhole at the front meant I was shit out of luck.

"Oh, you've lost your mind, Azreal," I screeched, pulling hard enough at my wrists that the skin burned. The smirk on his face was enough for me to do another series of kicks in his direction that I knew were futile.

"Still as stunning as ever, Eden" he said, licking his lips.

I kept my eyes on his face and off his body, but he didn't do the same. It was like he was memorizing every change in my body since we'd last seen each other. My hips were wider, my ass a little more full, my breasts heavier. But what really caught his interest was my hair. He loved it long and when I'd left I chopped it off, hoping I'd stop seeing him touching my strands every time I looked in the mirror.

"The short hair suits you," he continued when I didn't reply. My glare didn't stop him from talking. "We both knew this was inevitable. But, I am sorry about the loss of your friend."

I felt a sliver of hurt at his words that, I hoped, didn't show on my face. He took a chance, sliding a little closer to me, and I let him. I needed him close so I could hurt him.

"I was hoping you'd stay downstairs until I came for you, but I knew you wouldn't. That just means you get to stay here where I can see you," he whispered his words in my ear as he grabbed something off the shelf. "I'd trust you to behave, but we both know that's pointless."

I moved to knee him, but he expected it. He grabbed my thigh and wrenched it to the side and pulled me up, so I was straddling his hips. That's when his pelvis ground against mine. I opened my mouth to protest, and he shoved the silicone ball into my mouth and behind my teeth. I tried to move my head from his grip, but that delicious pleasure of him rocking against my core was both glorious and distracting. In three seconds, the gag was secured in my mouth, but that didn't stop his hands from shifting under me and finding their way into my pants.

We both groaned when he found out how soaked I was. Instead of exploring past my panties, he pulled his hand back before maneuvering my feet to the ground. His eyes met mine, and I hated his feral gaze almost as much as I hated myself for wanting him to finish what he started. Breathing hard, I sank to the ground, the restraints moving down the pole behind me.

"We'll continue this in the morning," he said, walking back to his bed and pulling the sheets over himself. He settled back in, ignoring the cold air that was flowing into the room.

I looked forlornly at the gun, far too far away. In my mind, I knew I was ready to shoot him. To take him out and finally be done with all of this. But when I squeezed my thighs tight, trying to curb the ache between them, I acknowledged that was wishful thinking. One look, one touch, one kiss—and I was parting my thighs, welcoming him back between them. The man was a dangerous killer, and I was wet. What did that say about me?

He was facing me, watching my every move like I was the most fascinating thing he'd ever seen. It was the same way he'd watched me before. But now I could see it for what it was: insanity. And, heaven help me, I kinda liked it.

"Fuck you," I said as concisely as I could.

"I missed you too," he muttered before closing his eyes, that smug smile still on his face.

I couldn't wait to wipe it off.

5

There was a crick in my neck from falling asleep on my arm, but I was grateful to wake up alone. A puddle of drool rested below my cheek, and I wiped it away on my shoulder as I looked around. The curtains were drawn in the room, but a cold wind pushed against them, flickering little bits of light against my face. I was nestled into a thick blanket that had been placed over me after I'd fallen asleep.

Sitting up, the blanket dropped and I crinkled my nose. Not only was I a prisoner, I smelled like I had taken up residence under an overpass. I needed a shower. And a drink. But I would've settled for that shotgun back so I could fill Az's stupid face with pellets.

His giant bed was tightly made with dark red sheets. We'd spent hours between those sheets, finding each other's bodies the night that I ran. He was able to touch parts of my spirit that I'd thought were out of reach. Hell, I'd walked sideways for two full weeks, and at one point I was sure I was going to feel him inside me forever.

And it had all happened there.

I stood, looking up to inspect the lock on the cuffs, but there was still no way to get the damn thing open. With the ball gag in my mouth, I couldn't yell for help, but I could bang the o-ring against the metal. So I did. The echoing was deafening, but once I built a rhythm, I didn't care. It was make noise or stay here and wait for him to come back.

After a few minutes, the door opened and Az breezed inside, coming to a stop in front of me. His hands were behind his back and I watched the green turtleneck stretch across his chest. In the daylight, I could see the light streaks of gray in his beard, and there was something more in his eyes that I couldn't read.

"I'd be lying if I said this wasn't exactly how I'd planned to keep you after you burned out the bloody clutch in my Noble." He leaned close, but not close enough to be in kicking range. Not that I'd have kicked him. I had to play nice to get what I wanted. And right this second that was free of these shackles and a shower.

Still, I couldn't help antagonizing him just a little. "Psycho," I mumbled against the gag.

He laughed before stepping forward and putting his hands out in front of him. "Before we start, I want to lay out the rules." He was watching me warily before he came closer. When I didn't protest, his hand came to my neck.

"No lying. No secrets. Not this time." His thumb traced a line to the soft leather strapped to my face. "Nod," he whispered, vulnerability clouding his words. I nodded.

"I know you've felt it. That ache. Give me a month. Let me remind you of us. Show you what it can be like with nothing between us." His eyes held mine while he traced my lips around the gag.

"I'm going to release you, and we're going to talk," he said, cautiously. I nodded, careful not to make any sudden moves. His fingers pulled at the leather holding the gag in place first, gently pulling it from my mouth. Next, he reached up and undid the cuffs one by one. Instinctively, I ran my hands over my wrists as he took a step back to place the cuffs down.

When he turned around, I was already reaching back for momentum, so my fist could fly at his face. I threw all of my weight behind the punch, and it landed across his jaw. He staggered back a few steps, holding his face in surprise.

I, on the other hand, immediately started shaking out my fist, convinced I'd broken something against his face. "Motherfuck. Jumping black Jesus. Ow! Ow. Ow."

Az looked up at me and laughed as he massaged his face. "I deserved that, I guess," he said, though his eyes sparkled with fury.

Despite his words, I took a step back, watching as he steadied himself and stood to his full height. "Are you going to rip out my intestines, too?" I asked.

The fury immediately left him as he pulled his hands back behind him, his face becoming the same careful mask. "I will never hurt you," he said, his eyes matching the sincerity in his tone.

"I lied to you," I said, lightly massaging my aching knuckles.

"I always knew who you were," he said. I gasped as he gave me a devious grin. "And I would *never* hurt you," he repeated, slowly. After a pause, he asked, "Are you afraid of me?"

"No," I answered, not sure who was more surprised, me or him. I was upset and confused, but I knew if he wanted to kill me, I'd have woken up upside down last night. My hand came to my neck as I stretched it left and right. "I'm not staying here a month. A week. That's enough time to fuck and get it out of our systems."

Az tilted his head and grinned. "Give me until Christmas. Twelve days." He moved forward, and his eyes scanned my body again, slowly like a caress. "And twelve nights." I knew what he was doing. But I also knew I could keep my sanity until Christmas.

"Fine," I agreed.

"That's the first and last time you ever put your hands on me in anger," he said, letting me see a little flicker of his rage.

Tilting my head to mirror his, I countered with, "That's the first and last time you ever drug me."

He smirked and held out his hand for me to shake. I held out my own and instead of shaking on our deal, he pulled my hurt knuckles to his mouth and kissed them lightly, leaving slow, lazy kisses along my skin. When he looked at me, the ferocious heat in his eyes made one thing clear—he planned to keep me past Christmas.

And I had to do everything I could to run before then.

6

We ate together in silence. It was odd being back here after all this time. The sitting room on the second floor was cozy and full of modern furniture. There was a small table in the adjoining sunroom and that's where we ate our early dinner.

My attention was on the grounds. Everything was lush and green as far as I could see. The city was so stacked on top of itself that the history was rich and complex. But, out in the country, there was nothing but wilderness. And that was something I hadn't seen much of growing up.

"What are you thinking about?" Az asked. I turned to see him watching me, sipping at a glass of water.

"How much I missed this country. And how you ruined some of that for me." The honesty seemed to surprise him. I'd never really been blunt before when I was playing the role of Jordan. She knew just what buttons to push and which to leave alone. But he'd asked for honesty and if that helped build the wall around my heart that I needed to abandon him and this world, I was okay with that.

He sat back in thought as I looked back out at the gardens down below us. The hedge maze was gone and in its place, there was nothing but a pond with a fountain, winking against the sun. Swans and ducks floated across the surface as someone walked toward them from the house carrying a bag. From the way the animals leapt from the water, I knew it had to be food. The worker started throwing out food and was promptly overrun as Az spoke, "Did I?" he asked.

"Lord Azreal. Part-time security expert, part-time serial killer. Given wealth and influence, he still dismembers victims in his basement," I said in my terrible British accent.

"Not victims," he clarified. Something in his tone made me turn to him. He pushed aside a bowl of prawn crackers and leaned forward.

"Interesting. What do you call them, then? Prey?"

"Offenders."

"What?" I asked, leaning away from him as he reached for my hand.

"The days will be for us. But the nights. The nights will be for work. My work," he clarified unnecessarily.

All the dumplings I'd just eaten shifted in my belly. He didn't... He couldn't... "You can't be serious."

"I promised you truth and transparency. You can tell me when it's too much, but I need you to understand it from the beginning to the end."

Everything at that moment felt slow. Like I was treading through a thick bog, too foggy to see in front of me. Was I supposed to move forward or backward? Did the direction even matter? I knew deep down that whatever path I chose, I was never going to be rid of Az. Not really.

"Offenders," I repeated, tilting my head and watching as his beautiful mouth turned down in a way that showed his disgust. Maybe I owed it to him, to what I'd felt for him, to understand what this was and why he did it.

I didn't give him a chance before because I was afraid it would make sense. That I'd be further ensnared by him. This was the opportunity to change that. And if I managed to get free from him this time, at least it would be with my eyes wide open.

"Okay," I said, grabbing a prawn cracker and snapping it in half and then in half again to give my hands something to do. "So, tell me," I said.

"Tonight," he replied, grabbing a cracker of his own.

Azreal led me to a bathroom on the second floor and left me to clean up. The shower was as hot as I could stand as I used a washcloth to scrub my skin. The bruises from the cuffs weren't bright, but I could feel them, hiding beneath my skin. I finger combed my hair, wincing at the knot from last night.

Sighing, I stayed under the water for much longer than I needed to. It felt good to wash everything away, to keep my focus on the present and not the past.

This wasn't quite the Az that I remembered. He was there, but not there. There was something between us that we'd been dancing around. Now I knew—it was the truth. If he'd known the whole time I was lying to him, he wouldn't have wanted to let me in. It was all starting to make more sense, and yet, it still made no sense at all.

I wrapped a fluffy towel around myself and wandered into the room. A pair of sweats were lying on the bed and I eyed them carefully, not sure his clothes would fit me. But it was that or nothing. I'd left my carry-on in the hotel. I'd packed it carefully in case I needed to abandon it to make a break for the airport. The only thing I needed was the pouch. So, dick first. Pouch and wallet, second. Escape, third.

Grabbing the sweatshirt, I pulled against the sides of the material and noticed that it had a lot of stretch. The suit fit well enough. I looked around the room and saw that it was sparse, but still slightly feminine. My room—no, my prison—was right next to Az's. When I moved toward the dresser, I saw a tablet with a sticky note.

Did I miss anything?

Picking up the tablet, I saw he'd spent a few hundred pounds on some things for me to wear. I rolled my eyes, seeing that some of the pieces were matching bra and panty sets. He fucking wished. I threw the tablet, and it thudded against the bed as I pulled a pair of thick socks onto my feet.

But, instead of getting up, I found myself falling back onto the duvet, relaxing into the comfort of the bed. My belly was full, and I was warm and clean. I looked back at the tablet and noticed that everything he'd picked out would fit. I balled up the note and threw it across the room as I exited out of the app.

There was another open tab, and, of course, my nosey ass looked. Familiar blue eyes were staring back at me. It was the man who'd begged me to save him. I yelped and covered my mouth. After getting over my shock, I checked the door before scrolling on the document.

Walter Grouse Sr.

40 years old.

No convictions.

Crimes include: elder abuse, blackmail, distribution of pornographic material filmed without consent, and desecration of a corpse.

The file was extremely detailed. He took jobs with charities that worked with the elderly to end the loneliness epidemic. He'd come into their homes, torture them, and in one instance they found semen on a dead woman's nightgown. There was evidence that she'd been asphyxiated.

That horrible human had terrorized these people when he was supposed to help them. I flipped through the pages, trying to see why he'd never been convicted, but all I saw was more and more evidence, including stills of images that had been found on a hidden hard drive in his house. One of which showed him dousing a very dead woman's face with cum.

My stomach roiled in disgust as I scrolled back up and looked at his face again. He'd been a monster. A true, honest to god, villain. When I put the tablet down, I couldn't get the image of that woman out of my mind. She couldn't even find peace in her death. He'd robbed her of it in her last moments and after.

That piece of shit deserved everything he got.

An hour later, Az found me staring out the window, watching the sun sinking towards the skyline. He sat silently beside me and fixed his gaze out at the hills. I was grateful he didn't say a word, didn't try and comfort me, he just sat beside me so that I wasn't alone.

After a while, I let my head fall against his shoulder as I sighed. "Tell me," I said, my eyes looking at the pink and gold sliver where the sun used to be.

"The scales must always balance," he said, his voice clear.

"And his scales said he deserved to be strangled with his own bowels?" I asked.

"I weigh their deeds against the world they've ruined. Do you believe that he didn't deserve death?" His hands were clasped tight in his lap. I picked one of them up, turning it palm up and tracing the lines there.

"Did you enjoy it?" I whispered.

"My hands are heavy but necessary," he replied, not answering the question.

I shut my eyes, trying to rid my brain of those images, and instead, I saw him strung up, his eyes pleading for mercy. For the first time, I wasn't conflicted by the idea of what I'd seen. It felt good to rewatch him die. I was silent for a few moments more, my fingers slowly tracing the lines of his palm.

"I can show you more," he said. "If you're ready."

Taking a breath, his unique scent surrounded me and gave me the comfort I didn't realize I needed to feel. Sitting up straight, I turned to see him looking over at me, his eyes full of something I couldn't quite figure out. Instead of trying, I pulled away from him.

"Okay," I replied, threading my fingers with his and letting him pull me up and guide me from the room.

His office was a few doors down from the sitting room on the second floor. He pulled out a chair and motioned for me to sit as he woke up his computer. The room was very sleek and modern, which contrasted with the old, drafty house. He moved his cursor over to a feather widget that looked like it was a part of his computer background and clicked.

The screen sprang to life with an overlay of Great Britain. Some areas were a brighter red than others and I leaned forward trying to make sense of what I was seeing. He zoomed in to where we were in Winchester, and I was surprised to see there was no red.

"The algorithm scans the internet and creates hot zones of activity," Az said before I could ask the question.

"And you built it to find people?" I asked.

Az scrunched up his face. "I didn't build it, but someone I trust did. I've been tracking a bar in Basingstoke. Once your delivery gets here, we're going to take a look around and see if we can spot anything."

"You're taking me with you?" I turned to look at him in disbelief.

"You saw the dossier. You understand now." He shrugged.

"But, I don't," I replied. "Well, I do. He was a despicable fucking monster. But why you? Why all this?"

He turned away from the computer and gave me a wry grin. "My family has upheld Ma'at for generations—not as a religion, but as a philosophy. Balance, justice, truth... these aren't just ideals to us. They're laws, ones the world too often forgets. I balance the scales."

I sat back, taking him in, trying to make sense of what he was explaining to me. "What happens when you get it wrong? You're judge, jury, and executioner—*you* are the scales— and you're not being fair," I said. "Justice wasn't ever meant to be found by one person alone."

"I weigh all my choices carefully, but the world isn't fair, Eden," he replied. "Where was fairness for their victims? I answer for a system that doesn't care about balance or fairness—only justice."

A chime rang through the house and Az stood. He leaned down and palmed my cheek. His features softened as he trailed his fingers across my skin. When his teeth sank into his lip, I knew he was stopping himself from doing something more.

"Ma'at isn't just about punishing the guilty—it's about preventing harm before it spreads." His lips came to my cheek, lingering for a moment before he turned and walked out of the office.

I sat, staring at the space that he'd just left, and tried to work through everything I'd learned in the last hour. When I grabbed the mouse, I scrolled across the screen. Some of the larger cities were bright red, but I brought my attention back to Winchester and the surrounding areas. Was he the reason there wasn't any red on this map?

The tight strands I'd held on to about Azreal being a murdering psychopath were fraying. Because, yes, he *was* a murdering psychopath, but there was something else there, something else reserved just for me. A lightness that showed that he wasn't all dark. But I wasn't willing to embrace the dark for him before...

Was I willing to now?

7

The drive to Basingstoke in Az's SUV was a quick twenty minutes. We left as soon as I changed into some of the clothes that were delivered. While the car was silent, it wasn't an uncomfortable one. He handled the small England roads much better than I had. He shifted with ease and relaxed against the seat. Seeing him like this, in control and confident, was fascinating to watch. He'd never seemed this relaxed around me before. Maybe now that everything was out in the open, he felt like himself for the first time.

I know I did.

The pub was bustling and brightly lit, but it was a Friday, so it wasn't at all a surprise. When I'd looked at the area, it looked like this was the busiest pub around here, and that tracked. A busy and loud three-room pub was the kind of place where you could easily blend in and lose track of people. I found two seats in a corner near the bar while Az headed to the counter and ordered us both ciders.

He came to the table with the bottles, and I smiled, seeing he'd grabbed the cider I loved. He shrugged off his coat and I grabbed it from him, placing it on top of the one he'd just bought for me near the window ledge.

There was something in the way that he was looking at me that had me squirming in my seat and leaning a little further away from him.

"So, you're not expecting twelve blow jobs for the clothes, are you?" I asked. He gave me a look before taking a sip of his beer. The silence was loaded, and I awkwardly shrugged. "Okay, bad joke," I said. "You don't like blow jobs."

He shook his head and tugged at one of my curls. "Eden."

Before I could stop myself, I asked what I'd been wanting to all day. "You knew the whole time?"

A sexy smile split his face. "The second you started researching me, the firm flagged it," he replied, taking a sip from his bottle and keeping an eye on the crowd.

"And you let me con you?" I took a sip from my own bottle.

"You didn't con me, though, did you?" I startled, but he kept talking. "When we talked, you were never Jordan, you were Eden."

Scrunching up my face, I leaned closer. "There's no way you could've known that."

"I didn't. Not until you talked about Sekhmet. Your mom published a paper on the Cult of Isis. Jordan was a trust fund baby. She wouldn't know anything about Sekhmet, would she?" He winked as he grabbed my thigh, giving it a squeeze.

His touch went straight to my swirling belly, and I wanted him to touch me higher.

"Since we're being honest, when you ran, well, you didn't take what you thought you did."

"I'm confused," I said, putting my bottle down.

He flashed me a smile before pulling out his keys and holding up the charm. It was one of the Greco-Roman gold coins I'd stolen and sold when I went home.

"Not real."

I reached for the keys, but he put it back in his pocket. "I got paid!" I half-screeched.

"You did," he said, taking another drink.

The money I needed to restart my life came from the man that I ran from.

My mouth fell open. "Why?" I was asking him that a lot. Maybe I was being obtuse, but no one just up and handed out that much money to someone stealing from them.

"I knew you'd be back," he said simply, reaching out and chucking beneath my chin, so I would close my mouth. "And I wanted you taken care of. Same reason there's a big tree in the great room."

I shivered and blinked hard before looking back toward the bar. My hormones had me ready to risk it all right then and there. Eye contact with him was too dangerous. And with the way, his smooth brown skin gleamed in the light, I was ready to rip that turtleneck off him and do unspeakable things. He sat for a moment, gazing out across the crowd, before he leaned close and grabbed my waist, scooting flush against me.

"You're afraid of what's inside you, Eden." His mouth came to my neck, his tongue darting out to taste my skin. I fought hard not to close my eyes and revel in the feel of having him close to me again. "That's why you ran." His teeth nipped, and I bit down on my lip, trying not to show how much he was affecting me. "But you're not running from you or from me again."

I whimpered as his nip became a bite and I felt it everywhere. My fingers fisted on the table and I took a second to find the words. "I'll run again if staying means becoming like you."

That earned a laugh that felt entirely too wicked. His hand around my waist teased the skin under my shirt along my back as it made its way towards my waist, grabbing and holding on to my abundant curves.

"You already are like me. You'll come to see it. And when you do, I'll be there to show you how perfect that makes you." His lips trailed up to my ear, catching the lobe as he whispered, "And I plan to swallow every inch of that perfection, body and soul."

My breath stuttered as my blood heated. I wanted nothing more than to feel him moving along my skin, filling me over and over, but I'd just watched the bartender turn his hand over a glass and hand it to a woman engrossed in her phone.

"Stop," I said, trying to pull away, but his hand on my thigh stopped me.

"We're here to watch, not intervene," he said.

I pulled away from him. "What?" the word was practically a screech, and a few people turned and looked towards me. He gave me a look, but let my thigh go, and I bounced out of my seat.

"Karen!?" I screamed across the room. The woman on her phone didn't look up, but several of the people around her did. I galloped and stumbled towards the woman, raising my voice even more. "Karen, is that you?" I adopted my best Long Island accent and grabbed the woman from behind, smacking the glass hard enough that it fell over, spilling alcohol all over her and the bar.

"Excuse me? Get your hands off me." She hissed, trying to free herself from my bear hug. I took a step back and looked down at her, letting my jaw go slack.

"You're not Karen," I replied, adding a drunken lilt to my words.

"I most certainly am not," she replied, standing and shaking her wet clothes. "Unbelievable!"

"Hey, it was an accident!" I felt an arm circle my waist and pull me backward.

"I told you it wasn't Karen, baby." Az's American accent wasn't bad, but it also wasn't very good.

"I thought it was," I said, turning to him. He was pissed. I looked back at the woman and said, "Shit, I'm sorry, honey."

"You and the missus need to go." The bartender said, looking at the disgruntled woman who was grabbing her purse to leave.

"Alright, keep your clothes on. I'll go." I let Az put my coat around my shoulders and lead me outside.

The weight of his stare on me was heavy as he pushed me through the street to where we'd parked. Our pace was quick and silent. When I tried to slow down, Az just moved us faster. I knew I'd upset his precious balance, but I didn't give a fuck. There was no way that I was going to let that bartender drug that woman and do whatever he had planned. We came to a stop on my side, but instead of opening the door, he yanked my back to his front, sandwiching me between him and the car.

"You are infuriating," he whispered as he moved my hair to the side and dragged his lips across my skin.

"Eat me." I hissed, feeling my pussy twinge.

His mouth opened and sucked so hard that my knees buckled. I grabbed on to the car door to keep myself upright as his hand moved up my side, finding my breast. Reaching back, my hand found him hard in his jeans, and we moaned in unison as I traced the outline of him.

I'd had sex since I'd run from him in some desperate bid to get him out of my system, but nothing felt as good as he did at that moment. I was ready to free him from his jeans—ready to feel the soft skin of him in my hand—when he opened the door and pushed me inside.

My leg was barely inside before he snapped the door shut and leaned against it. My breath was coming fast, and I could feel my heart beating in my clit. Time apart hadn't dulled the fire between us, and I was more than ready to fuck the shit out of him for everyone to see.

After a few minutes, he was sliding into the driver's seat. He peeled out of the spot and started to drive us back towards Winchester.

"You didn't seriously expect me to let him drug that woman?" I asked, watching his grim expression.

When he didn't reply, I figured he needed some incentive to talk. My hand moved his coat to the side and grabbed his thigh. He still wasn't talking, so I brought my fingers to his zipper and pulled it slowly down. He huffed out a breath but didn't make a move to stop me as I unbuttoned his pants and freed his dick from its confines.

What started out as a game, turned into something more when I saw him. My mouth watered as his large head popped free, followed by the rest of his length. His eyes were on the road and not on me. I slid the seat belt over to the side and leaned closer to him, my fingers ghosting over his velvety skin. Taking a breath, I leaned down and swallowed the length of him.

"Jesus," he hissed as I hollowed my cheeks and pulled more of him into my mouth. I bobbed, flattening my tongue and feeling his dick leap in my mouth. Breathing through my nose, I tried to relax my throat to pull him all the way down. He tasted like sweat and warm skin. Pre-cum was coating my tongue with a tang that made me bob my head faster. My hand fisted at his base and moved in concert with my lips.

I sucked harder as I heard his breathing increased. His hands wound into my hair as he tried to pull me off him, but I just moved faster, loving the control I had over him. When I hummed against him, he jerked the wheel and the car bounced a bit on an uneven road before coming to a hard stop.

My thumb undid the seatbelt as he pushed his seat back and leaned forward to grab my jaw. His eyes were wild, but all fury was gone from them. Lust was pulsing between us and the tension was heavy. When the pad of his thumb traced my lip, I felt it everywhere.

"Come here."

He helped me over the console and my thighs fell on either side of his. His hand found the back of my neck and pulled me into him. There wasn't a moment of hesitation when his lips attacked mine, holding me tight to him as he tongue-fucked my face. I pulled at my own pants, and he helped me yank them down my hips.

I felt like I was going to explode when he cupped my mound. His teeth nipped at my lips as he caressed my skin, flooding my body with so much pleasure that I felt like I was going to unravel. I breathed into his mouth, trying to calm down as pleasure coiled tight in my belly, ready to snap.

His hand was still against my skin, and I moved against him, trying to get him to touch me where I needed him. I was alight. My hand found his jaw and I tilted his face so I could see him.

"Touch me," I hissed, angling my hips and chasing his hand that was just out of reach.

"Ask me nicely," he whispered, his smug smile shining bright in the dark car.

My hands went to his turtleneck, holding him to his seat. He licked his lips and I leaned forward, my tongue taking the same trail that his had just taken.

"Really?" I exhaled against his lips, before pushing myself up against his chest and running my gushing slit up and down his shaft. "Well, I guess we should go."

I tried to swing my thigh off him when he buried three fingers into my pussy, angling forward and back.

"That's what I thought," he moaned as my eyes started to roll up in my head. His fingers thrust up and found a solid rhythm. The sounds I made as he pushed up into me—the wet suction of my greedy pussy—bounced around the car. He moved his fingers in and out of me in a way that made me feel like nothing else existed in the world but us. I leaned back and rolled my hips with him, my orgasm coming faster than I expected.

His thumb brushed my clit and I cried out, jerking harder against him. He grabbed my jacket and yanked me forward and rolled rough circles as his tongue matched his rhythm. When his teeth found my lip, I exploded, shuddering against him as he milked my pussy. Twisting his fingers, they pulled back to lightly graze my g-spot and my hands weaved into his hair as I moaned into his mouth, my thighs still shaking as pleasure shot through my body.

I found his length underneath me and fisted it, pulling up and down in time with his strokes into me.

"The first one was free. You're not getting another until you ask me nicely," his words were spoken against my jaw, and I couldn't stop the moans surging from my lips.

"Make me cum," I whispered, pulling back to spit on his dick.

"That's better. You want me to make you cum? What's the magic word?" he asked, pumping into my fist.

"Fuck me and stop teasing me," I groaned as his strokes set me on fire.

He hummed for a moment before those sure circles returned to my clit and I clamped down on him, my pussy full and gushing. When I came, it was on a long groan against his mouth as I kept my tight grip on him. He fisted my hand over him, and we stroked his dick three more times before he came with a groan, stuffing his cum soaked hand into my mouth while he licked my juices from his fingers.

My tongue sucked before I stopped and looked down at his now semi-erect dick. The smile on his face was absolutely infuriating, and I was regretting our agreement about violence because my horny ass was ready to fight. Batting his hand away from my mouth, I frowned down at him.

"Azreal," I said, pointedly looking at his dick.

"He likes it when you ask nicely," he replied, shrugging.

I took a deep breath and tried not to think about the thrumming ache between my thighs or the fact that I was next in line for the log ride and that motherfucker was shut down for maintenance.

I rose off him, ignoring my aroused, dripping pussy and my burning thighs. All that hovering and acrobatics my big ass just did, and he didn't even fuck me. Silently, I buckled my pants and put on my seatbelt and looked out the foggy window.

The drive back to the manor was short. He didn't pull into the garage, and I hopped out the second he put the car into park. I was standing by the door as he waved his key-ring over the fob and opened it.

I didn't realize I didn't hear him behind me until I got to the top of the stairs and the SUV engine started back up. When I turned around, he was driving away. Before I even got the chance to yell at him.

Dickhead.

8

December 15th, 2024

"Eden," Az's voice pulled me awake, and I grumbled angrily, turning away from him. "Eden," he called again.

"I swear to every single deity, if you're waking me up to get pussy, I'm drop-kicking you clean out that fucking window," I replied, not opening my eyes.

"You came," he said behind me. I flipped over and pinned him with a glare that very clearly said, *don't piss me off*. He stood by my bed, still wearing what he'd left the house in. I'd changed back into his sweats before going right to sleep, swaddled in every blanket I could find. When he saw the murderous look on my face, he held up his hands. "Okay, you're right. That was too far."

"What do you want, Az?" I grumbled, settling back into the warm spot beneath the covers.

"I have something to show you." That grin was gone, and in its place was the same mask he'd worn when I was grifting him. I sat up in the bed and looked him over. There was nothing out of place, but something was different.

"Where?" I asked.

"You know where," he answered.

A jolt shot through me. He meant the torture room. There was someone in his dungeon, and he wanted me down there with him as he dispensed justice.

"Azreal, I don't know," I said, swallowing against the hole that felt like it had worn its way through my stomach.

"Please?" he asked, holding out his hand for me. Reconnaissance was one thing, but this—what he was asking—I wasn't sure I could do this. "You're welcome to leave the room at any point," he whispered.

There was a pull. A strange fascination was making me want to say yes. It wanted to know more about the bartender. About the hotspot of activity that Az discovered in the bar and how we could help the victims of this man.

"At any point?" I asked, watching his hand warily.

"At any point," he repeated.

I crawled out of bed and threw on some shoes. When I found his hand with mine, he gave it a light squeeze.

"I'll give you some dick the next time you ask," he said as he walked us out the bedroom door.

"Oh, fuck off, Az," I hissed. The arousal may be gone, but I was still grumpy as hell.

We walked through the cold ass manor in silence. Each step that brought us closer to the wine cellar made me feel nauseous. It was a mix of both unease and excitement. My throat got sweaty. It was like my body knew the joy I felt about the man getting what he deserved was wrong. I tried not to think too hard about it as we walked through the wine cellar. Az pushed on a panel that opened the door to the dungeon.

The bartender was strapped to the chair, his eyes were uncovered. Layers of tape were stacked around his mouth, all the way around his brown, sweaty hair. He couldn't have been more than thirty. His pupils were the size of saucers, and I could barely see the brown of his irises. Azreal shrugged off his coat and placed it on a hook, following it with his turtleneck.

I gasped, seeing the tattoo across his chest. One of Ma'at's wings was open wide, but the other was cradling Sekhmet. The exact version of her that had been on the book he'd given me. I didn't have time to think about it because he started talking to the bartender.

"Rand Christopher. Twenty-four years old. No convictions. Do you know how many women you are suspected of drugging?" Az said, oblivious to my gaze fixed on the Sekhmet permanently etched above his heart.

The man mumbled, and even I could see that he was lying. The sweat pouring from his brow and the pleading look he gave me said that he knew he was fucked.

"Twenty-two," Az said. "Is that right?"

Rand shook his head vigorously. I watched in fascination as tears filled his eyes as he looked at me.

"You're going to answer every question I pose truthfully, and maybe you'll live," Az said. "You won't remember a thing because you're high on your own supply. But, if you lie, you'll find things get a bit more complicated for you."

Az walked away and grabbed some shears from the wall. That's when I saw the table full of implements. Knives, screwdrivers, scalpels, a bone saw, and even what looked like a pen with a metal tip. And, of course, the curved knife that looked like a scythe.

When he spotted Az grabbing something off the table of tools, he freaked out, pulling against the binds on his hands and feet as he tried to escape. Az didn't even look like he noticed as he walked slowly toward the man and gently sliced through the tape on his mouth before pulling at it and taking some skin with it. Blood welled up on his lips, but that didn't stop the pleading.

"Please, I promise, I didn't do what you think I did. Please, please. Let me go." The babbling was quick, and he was looking directly at me and I looked over at Az who gave me a head tilt.

"He's asking the questions. Is twenty-two right?" I asked. Az smirked at me as he walked back over to the table to grab the bone saw while slipping the plastic pen into his jean pocket.

"I—I never counted. I swear. I never counted. I don't know." Tears fell from his eyes. I believed him. But he didn't deny it.

"We're going to take this slow, Rand. Do you deny drugging those people?" Az asked, holding the saw against his thigh.

Rand shook his head aggressively. "No. I did. I did it," he sputtered. "But that was all I did, I swear."

"You didn't rape them?" The words came out before I could stop them. My voice sure and strong, a contrast to the knot of emotions welling in my throat.

"No, I just, they pay me to help," he was sobbing now, his eyes glued to the saw in Az's hand.

"Who?" Az asked.

"Please, mate, I just drugged the drinks."

"And you'll receive your punishment for that. As long as you tell the truth." Az placed a gentle hand on the man's shaking shoulder. After a moment, Az patted him twice. "Names?"

"There are these twins, the last name is Grayson, with an 'a'. They're northern. Big blokes."

"One last question. Did you know what these men were doing?" Az's gaze was hawkish.

Rand stammered, his eyes jumping from me to Az and back again. He knew alright.

"But I didn't take the girls. I didn't hurt them. I told them to sleep it off in the back office, and they would just disappear. That's all, I swear."

Az nodded as he looked at me, trying to see if I agreed that he was being truthful. I nodded back.

"Okay. Thank you for your honesty. I'm going to take your hands and let you be on your way," Az explained.

Before Rand could even process the words, the automatic saw had already started and was tearing through his flesh. As the saw cut the skin and muscle, it made a slushing sound and after the shock wore off, Rand let out a blood-chilling scream that was much louder than the saw.

Gooey crimson and torn muscle fragments splattered everywhere as the saw began milling through the bone. The screaming stopped just as his wrist fell to the floor. Blood squirted, and I moved just in time to miss the majority of it.

Az grabbed the pen from his pocket and began pressing the pen to the profusely bleeding appendage. My mouth had fallen open sometime into the spectacle and hadn't closed since. Rand had blissfully passed out the second his right hand became his only hand. My eyes couldn't look away from the charred stump. The smell of burnt flesh hung heavy in the air, a mix of copper, barbecued meat, and something that was similar to leather.

"Be a dear and hand me the smelling salts from the table," Az was covered in blood as he meticulously worked zapping the flesh, cauterizing the wounds.

I walked numbly over to the table and opened a box from the local pharmacy. The small package was in my hand as I headed back over to Az, but I didn't hand it to him.

"Wait," I said. "Where's the mercy? Ma'at wasn't just about punishment. She was about balance. Is this balanced?"

Az looked from me to Rand's right hand. He placed the pen in Rand's lap as he turned to me. "He willingly took part in the torture of women, some who we have yet to locate. You know what that means?"

I stepped forward and placed the smelling salts in his bloody hand, trying not to feel the slick warmth dripping from it. Swallowing against the tickle in my throat, I said, "I do. But, don't you think people can change?" I asked, looking down at the unconscious man.

"I do," he replied softly, closing his hand around the salts. "But if even one woman was trafficked because he drugged her, his capacity for change does nothing to undo the trauma."

Az turned back to Rand, putting the smelling salts under his nose. He woke with a start and immediately started screaming again. I stepped back as the bone saw started back up. Something in my head was screaming to walk away, begging me to find the keys and save myself from the abyss clouding me, but I couldn't help but stand rooted in fascination as Az finished the job he'd started.

The screaming was a little much, but Rand passed out much quicker this time, as the muscles practically melted under the saw. As disgusting as the process was, Az wasn't torturing the man, he was doling out the punishment that he'd decided fit the crime, no more and no less. Cauterizing the wounds would stop the man from bleeding to death. And he'd never get the chance to drug any woman's drink ever again.

That was the balance that Az was looking for. The justice he craved. It was hard to comprehend, but I understood.

He turned to me, seeing the blood splattered on his sweats, and sighed, "I'll get you a fresh pair. Go wash up. And mind the blood as you go," he said, looking down at my shoes.

I backed up, watching as Az grabbed the hands and chucked them in to a metal bin in the corner like he was on the free throw line. He was absolutely fucking insane. And maybe I was too because I smiled a tiny bit at the sight as I turned to walk back upstairs to take a shower and take my ass back to sleep.

9

When I fell asleep, I expected my dreams to be haunted by screams and blood, but they weren't. I slept long and hard, cuddled into the warmth of the bed. There were more blankets at the foot of the bed when I woke up, and I tried not to smile at the idea of Az bringing me every single one in the manor. I got up, pulled on a sweater, and grabbed the trash bag with the sweats.

I wandered into the kitchen and saw a couple startle at the sight of me. The woman I recognized from feeding the ducks, but I hadn't seen the man before. I opened my mouth to introduce myself when the man grabbed the bag from my hands.

"I'll take that, Miss."

Without another word, he disappeared. I turned to the woman who was smiling at me. "The fridge is full of anything you could want. You missed breakfast, but there's a plate for you in the stove." She turned away and left me standing in the kitchen alone, confused as hell.

My eyes scanned the room and found the red blinking light staring at me from the door. After last night, I should absolutely run. Not just from Azreal, but from myself. I watched a man get sawed apart. The amount of blood that splattered across the ground, falling like heavy raindrops, did nothing to me. I didn't care that that man suffered.

Because he was complicit.

Ma'at was about bringing order and balance to the chaos of the world, and that is what Az was doing. Was his way also chaotic? Sure. But I learned a long time ago that it's important to speak a mark's language to get through to them.

People like Rand, they feed the chaos. They know what they're doing is wrong, and they do it anyway. Their moral compass is broken, and talking to them like they're regular humans wouldn't work. Speaking in violence, though, that would. And that's what he'd done. He used the same drugs that Rand used on women to take something from him.

I grabbed the plate from the stove and popped it into the microwave, eating alone while I stood in the kitchen, watching the birds flittering around outside the window. When I was done, I dropped my plate into the sink and turned to see if there was anyone else around. They hadn't come back since they'd disappeared, and that seemed to be by design. I walked out towards the foyer and looked at the tree and mountain of presents.

Instead of breezing past, I walked over, feeling the weight of the glass ornaments against my hand. I tried to picture Lord Azreal on his tippy-toes decorating the tree, and I snickered. When I looked down, my eyes caught my name on one of the presents. Frowning, I leaned closer, looking at all of the presents piled beneath the tree.

Each and every one had my name on it. My hand covered my mouth as my eyes went wide, and I blinked back tears. There were dates on them. Some were a few years old, but the one closest to me was dated for today. I stepped back and looked down at the proof that I'd never been far from his mind when I'd run. He'd spent the last two years collecting things for me, knowing that I'd be back.

They had my name on them, but I wasn't ready to look inside or acknowledge how full my chest felt, knowing that I was in his thoughts as much as he had stayed in mine. A few deep breaths and two tears later, I felt better. That's when I decided to hunt the man down that seemed to be doing his best to stay out of my way this morning.

I was wandering the second floor when I saw him typing on a laptop in the sitting room. A part of me was afraid that I'd be repulsed or horrified by him after seeing him at work last night. But he still looked like Azreal. Sexy as sin with his crimson turtleneck and soft skin. I allowed myself to take him in as he typed. His brow furrowed a bit like he was deep in thought, but there were no other signs of stress on his face.

All the research I'd done on him showed a temperate man who had a passion for the arts and a love for all things literature. Nothing mentioned family traditions, Egyptian mythology, and a dick that was made to make women tremble. But all of that was who he was. I fell in love with the first man, but the second was so driven, so practiced and determined, that I wondered what it would be like to fall in love with him too.

When he saw me arrive, he closed the computer and that line of worry on his face disappeared into a blinding smile as he patted the other side of the couch. It was like he'd been waiting for me to come find him.

"Good morning. Please, sit," he said, placing his computer on the table. As I sat, he cleared his throat and turned. "How are you feeling?" he asked.

"Fine. Did you order your staff to run from me?" I tilted my head as he laughed.

"Are you telling me you wouldn't try to convince them to let you out?" He was serious as hell beneath the laughter. And he was also right. If I'd had the chance, I would've convinced them to open the door. Would I have left? That was the million-dollar question. But a girl likes having options.

"I guess you got me there," I laughed, hitting my thighs and leaning forward. "What are you doing?"

"Nah, you've changed the subject twice," he said, his fingers finding mine and squeezing. "How are you?" he asked again, his gaze pointed.

"I'm... fine." I repeated.

"We promised honesty. Last night must have been a lot for you," he said low, bringing my hand to his lips and grazing the skin.

"What happened to the days being for us?" I asked, leaning in to his touch.

"You're right. The days are for us," he placed a wet kiss on the inside of my wrist. "And right now, we have someplace to be. Let's get ready."

"Don't you have a job?" I asked, frowning as he pulled me to stand.

"If I couldn't take a vacation from my company, I'd be a terrible business owner," he replied before pulling me forward for a chaste kiss. "Now, put on something warm, we're going to the city."

Hours later, we stepped out of the Tate Modern and started making our way up towards Waterloo. Azreal hadn't let my hand go since we stepped on the train out of Winchester, and I was glad for it. I'd missed the feel of his skin on mine, the way his spirit radiated when we talked about nothing and everything. He was the only man who had ever got to know me before ever trying to fuck me, and that made him special—made our bond special.

I was staring at the water when he slowed to a stop and pulled my back to his front so we could watch the Thames rush by.

While I stared at each Picasso, like I was trying to memorize each brush stroke and color choice, he murmured random facts that he seemed to know about every piece we stopped in front of. It was a reminder that Azreal was a Lord and that his family had been rich for generations. But he never showed it. He didn't act posh or pretentious towards other people, every person got some degree of a kind smile or nod from him.

The first time I noticed, we'd just met, and he almost ran into someone walking behind him. The moment he realized the man was unhoused, he offered to buy him a cuppa and some lunch. I stood with the man while Az nipped into the coffee shop in front of us.

"It's not often I see such kindness," the man whispered to me.

I gave him a smile as Az turned from the counter and looked towards me and the man. "Yeah, I know," I'd replied.

As Az's arms wrapped around my belly, he found that familiar spot that seemed to be made just for him. He found his way past the collar of my coat as he inhaled the scent of my skin and sighed.

"I missed you," he said, tightening his hold.

"I missed you, too," I mouthed, afraid that saying the words aloud would pull me deeper into the chaos. Sitting there with the sounds of the surrounding city, I let myself believe that for a moment, I was just Eden, and he was just Azreal, and none of the darkness was threatening to pull us apart. When I finally got my voice to work, I changed the subject, trying to think of anything but the way everything about him felt right.

"I can't believe how much you know about art."

"It was my father." His words hung between us. I'd heard all about his late mother and the summers he'd spent in Sudan, but he never talked about his father. I gave him space to find the words. "Once he confirmed I was truly his son, he did everything he could to make me worthy of the King name. Tutors and a private boarding school, all of it leading right to Oxford." He spoke against my skin, his tone measured, but I knew he still felt the sting of it.

"You wanted to be the best for him," I whispered as a chilly gust of wind swept past us.

"I didn't realize I'd never be the heir he wanted until I was much older. When I turned fifteen, *abo* called me back to Sudan to watch my first judgment. It's been my duty since I turned eighteen. I don't remember my life without it guiding me."

I digested his words, thinking of a young version of him thrust into the role of judge, jury, and executioner. He buried our hands into my coat pockets. "That sounds very lonely," I said, leaning my head against his shoulder.

"It was—until a woman trying to steal from me talked about Sekhmet like a friend she'd had for centuries." His stubble rubbed along the back of my neck and I tried to wiggle away. "Now I have to convince her to come with me to the little breakfast place we found near Hampton Court Palace."

"I heard that she doesn't mind a good breakfast, but she did say something about a cat café—"

"You and this bloody cat café—"

"It's the cat café or letting me drive that little sporty car covered under a tarp."

His hands were out of my jacket and feeling the weight of my breasts as he spoke right in my ear. "I still haven't forgotten about the ten thousand pounds I spent on a new clutch or my pain and suffering. You'll never get behind the wheel of one of my cars again."

Turning in his hold, I put my arms around his neck as he frowned down at me.

"You're sure?" I asked, giving him a teasing smile as my fingers danced along his skin.

"Devious," he groaned, eyes closing as I traced underneath the collar of his coat. I let my touch move to his ears before framing his face. I wanted to memorize every part of him. This openness was new and thrilling, and I wanted more of it. But some of our past was still burrowed beneath my skin, making me feel uneasy. My thumbs traced his lips.

"You understand why?" I asked, changing the subject back to the night that I'd run. He knew what I was asking and his eyes opened, a soft gaze finding mine.

"Of course." He traced the line of my nose. "Do you feel like running, now?" he asked.

I answered truthfully. "Not today."

"Good." He pulled me up the small distance to his lips for a kiss. "If we were at home, you'd be half-naked."

I laughed against him, and he swallowed each exhale with his lips. "If we were in your manor, I'd be buried under two hundred pounds of blankets."

"I guess I'll have to do something about that if I want to keep you." He nuzzled my cheek with his ice cube of a nose.

"How romantic." I gave a dramatic half swoon. A swat came to my butt, and I was grateful for all the layers I was wearing.

"It's romance you want? Okay." His hand grabbed mine, and he pulled me towards the train station. Suddenly, I was both nervous and nauseous at the same time. Something told me I wasn't ready at all for what I just started.

10

I awoke to a heavy weight on top of my blankets. I groaned in protest as Az grumbled back. It was still dark out, and I couldn't see much in the room, but with the four blankets on top of me, I was finally feeling a little warmer. So much so that I'd lost my sweatpants in the night and my bare legs were rubbing against the sheets.

"Why are you in here?" I whined, trying and failing to escape the prison I'd made for myself.

"I wanted to be near you." The raw honesty stopped my wiggling.

"Oh." I don't know why that surprised me, or why it had my tummy flipping around. Yesterday had felt like the start of something between us, something raw and honest. But when we got back we ate a quick dinner in the kitchen before we came upstairs and said goodnight.

A part of me wanted something to happen, wanted to lose myself in him, but it didn't feel like the right moment.

He'd been quiet and introspective since we'd talked about his family. I was okay with that because I was trying to make sense of him as a young kid trying his best to gain his father's approval but knowing he'd never be the fair-skinned child the bastard wanted.

As he walked us up the stairs, he held my hand tight, as if grounding himself, before leaving me at my room door with a kiss on my cheek.

And now he'd found his way into my room.

"How do you decide on a punishment?" I asked, glad that I didn't have to look at those eyes that stripped my soul bare.

"I've got a system, but the algorithm helps," he said on a yawn as his fingers moved into my hair and slowly massaged my scalp.

"Have you ever taken it too far?" My thoughts went to the images I'd seen in that file. I didn't know if I could see that every day and not funnel my rage into every judgement.

"Yes. I'm just glad that you didn't see me fall when his intestines tore. He was terrified, though, so I guess it was worth it."

I froze, trying to give my brain a minute to catch up.

"Wait, you're telling me the image that has haunted me for years wasn't even how he died. And that it didn't even work, and you fell?" I guffawed and that turned into a giggle. After thirty seconds, I was crying, my stomach was cramping, and I was really pushing him off me because I couldn't breathe.

I managed to get a hold of myself after I grabbed my sides and leaned forward. Once the cramping passed, I caught him looking at me. Looking didn't feel like an accurate description, it was like he was seeing me for the first time, his gaze bouncing over me like he was trying to memorize every inch of me.

Both of us clearly wanted each other, but we were toeing the line. I didn't want to fall deeper into the darkness that I knew clung to him. And he was treating me like I was some skittish deer in the forest, ready to bolt at the slightest sign of danger.

"What?" The word came out breathy.

"You are—perfect," he said, awe in his tone and in the way his eyes lit up as his face searched mine.

"Really? I'm a thief. And a hoodlum. And a terrible baker. Never let me near flour, sugar and eggs. I'm liable to burn this manor down. On the flip side, I'd probably finally be warm as I turned into a briquette." I was babbling. I'd never been great with compliments. A bitch knew she was great, but when someone else said it, I couldn't handle it.

"Are you done?" The little line appeared on his forehead and I rolled my eyes.

"Az—"

"You are perfect for *me*. The way you shine illuminates some of my darkest shadows." Reverence coated his words and I could see the sincerity of them on his face. He gave me a half smile as he continued, "You're also a brilliant grifter, even though you chose a man specializing in cybersecurity to con." My mouth fell open, and he gave his shoulders the smallest shrug. Oh, this fool had jokes.

"That's not fair, the internet didn't say anything about your company. Or you," I said in a low voice.

He trailed his fingers along the length of my jaw before he gave my nose a boop. "It says that because I want it to." He laughed as I shoved his hand away.

"Well, now I know to be on the lookout for serial killers when I find my next mark."

"I'll help with that." The confidence in his tone was infuriating.

"Twelve days," I reminded him. "And you can't just invite yourself into my next grift."

"Imagine how much easier it would be if you had my resources," he said. I tried to reply, but he pressed his finger against my lips, "Before you say no, I think I owe you something."

He pushed away from me and did a perfect dive underneath the covers. When his hand gripped my neck and pulled my lips to his, I didn't fight him. We'd been playing this game for too long. Teasing touches and long stares weren't enough. I'd been hesitant because I knew falling into bed with him again would lead me to a version of myself I wasn't ready to really see.

But that version of me was the one that welcomed everything about Azreal. I needed him to fill me. To take every bit of that passion and lust and throw me into the bliss that both of us craved. My hands found his waist and pulled his pants past his ass, I squeezed it tight, feeling the heat of his body against mine. I sighed into his kiss as his tongue teased mine.

A small part of my brain was screaming about a toothbrush and a morning pee, but as my fist closed around his erection, all I could think about was him thrusting in to me so hard that I forgot my name and where I was from.

Fingers traced my stomach, feeling every dip and curve as he pulled my gown up to my neck. Every single touch sent me higher as his mouth devoured mine, leaving me no choice but to breathe when he allowed it. I was lightheaded when he finally released my mouth and brought his lips down to my breasts. Instead of tonguing my nipples, he chose a spot right above it and sucked the sensitive skin into his mouth.

I arched into his touch as my fist holding his dick started to move up and down. His foreskin gliding across his large mushroom head. Just the feel of him covering me had me so close to orgasm, I wondered if I could come this way. I didn't have to worry long. His hand found its way to my dripping slit as his mouth marked me in a way that only he had ever done. The light touch was enough for me to lean up and rub my clit against his hand.

He moaned before moving his thigh into my pussy while he and surrounded my throat with his wet hand. My hips writhed against him as the pressure deep in my belly was about to explode. His thumb caressed my pulse point as his dick jumped against my abdomen.

"Cum all over me, princess. We're going to drench these sheets."

I moved my hips in a circle, groaning as my orgasm drew close. Teeth tugged at my nipple, steadily increasing in pressure. That was all I needed to explode. Two fingers entered me and stroked up, leaving me shuddering and begging.

"Please." Became the only word in my vocabulary, and I was putty in his hands.

"You love this, don't you?" he asked. All I could do was nod as his fingers plundered my sensitive walls, making me holler.

"Oh? That seems like the perfect spot." He raised up a bit and placed his knee on my thigh before he moved his fingers in and out, right on my gspot. My body convulsed. The glutinous sounds my pussy was making had him moaning right along with me. An orgasm stole my breath and had me arching off the bed.

But he didn't stop. He added another finger. All three pistoned in and out of me so hard and fast that I felt like the oxygen had been pulled from the room. I gasped, trying to find more air as another orgasm rocked me and pressure built in me.

"Breathe," he encouraged.

I was incapable of thought. There was nothing left to do but feel, and I felt every single stroke inside of me. Every brush against my skin. The way his hands held on to my stomach for leverage. I tried and failed to move with his thrusts when he chuckled.

"Just take it. You're almost there," he whispered.

He was right. My next orgasm wasn't far away. When I came, the pressure came with a gush of liquid and a groaning moan so intense that my throat burned and tears filled my eyes. The fingers in me slowed their assault, and I felt the sudden urge to burst into tears. I swallowed them as I fought against the involuntary shuddering that wracked my body.

Settling himself between my thighs, he positioned himself at my entrance, slowly moving up and down before pushing his fat tip into me. He hissed, slowly working himself in before stopping and laying on my chest, taking a few deep breaths of his own.

"You still with me?" he asked.

I didn't have the strength to reply, but what I did do was clench down on him.

"Fuck," he said, before filling me completely.

The feeling of his sack smacking my ass made me feel like a sex goddess. I clenched again, and whatever tether of control Az was holding broke. Pulling out, he surged forward, grabbing my thighs so tight I knew they'd be marked in the morning. Each time he surged forward, I squeezed him tight.

Expletives rolled off his tongue as sweat coated his forehead and chest. The deeper he drove into me, the more guttural I sounded. Words were literally impossible. It was like base instinct took over and all I wanted to do was fuck and come. I met each of his thrusts so hard that he almost bounced out of me more than once. When he pulled out and came all over my chest, I grabbed at his dick, stroking it, rubbing it around in the mess that he'd made.

His face was a mask of pleasured pain as he watched my hand draw out his cum. As he softened, he gave me a look that said he wasn't through with me yet. And everything in me was pleased my that fact.

"Turn over," he ordered. I flipped, the cum on my breasts sticking to the sheets as I laid flat. "On your knees." I obeyed and was rewarded with his fat tongue stroked directly into my pussy.

Moaning into the pillow, I laid as much of my body down as I could, opening my thighs to give him more room. His tongue swirled around my clit and I shuddered. For a moment, he pulled away, and I felt the pillow at my face yanked away.

"Keep singing those carols for me," he whispered in my ear as his tongue and lips worked their way down my back. I arched into his touch, wanting his tongue right where I needed him.

When he reached my pussy, he wasn't timid. He devoured me. Between the noises I was making and the slurping and sucking filling the room, I was gushing on his face and screaming into another orgasm, ready for more.

"I think you can do better," he mumbled around me as his hands spread my cheeks open and his tongue fucked in and out of my pussy. Fisting the sheets, I rode his tongue, fucking back against him, eager and thirsty for more. I was so close to cumming when his thumb found my puckered hole and pushed inside. Moaning against the intrusion, I didn't have a moment to think or breathe before his fat dick replaced his tongue.

I threw it back. Every muscle in my body was screaming, my face was hot, and my lungs and throat were worn out, but the sounds coming from me were unrecognizable as I came so hard around his dick that I felt more liquid gushing down my thighs. He fucked me through the orgasm, his pace relentless, and I couldn't catch my breath.

The dizzy euphoria was clouding my mind and suddenly, I was weightless. My body fell to the mattress and everything went black.

A cold, wet feeling woke me up, and I batted it away. I was getting obliterated, and then I woke up on my back. I'd passed out. He'd fucked me so good that my body couldn't keep up. I was both impressed and absolutely horrified. I squinted against the bright light that he'd turned on and moved my hand up, hitting a naked chest.

"Stop it," Az ordered.

After another try, I opened my eyes to see him, still naked as the day he was born, dick softly swinging as he leaned over me. There was concern in his eyes, but that didn't stop the arrogant square of his shoulders or the little smile that lit up his face and showed off the just-fucked color in his cheeks.

"You certainly keep me on my toes," he whispered, laughter heavy in his tone.

I didn't laugh with him because I was praying for the ground to swallow me up. I'd just come so many times that I was probably one glob of saliva away from becoming a dehydrated husk. Lightning, a meteor, a discarded space station toilet seat, please use anything to take me clean out, universe. It was my time. There was nothing left for me. My eyes must've shown the absolute mortification I felt because he leaned down and gave me a soft kiss.

"This is so embarrassing," I moaned, my throat feeling like it had been rubbed with sandpaper.

"It's my new badge of honor." Lifting the towel from my breasts, he threw it onto the nightstand. "Now move over so we can get a few more hours of sleep."

I moved into the center of the bed and Az hit the light and moved in beside me. After a moment, he shoved the blankets off his side and tucked them over me. His cute little comment did little to ease my mortification. But I knew he would only double down if I gave him the chance. So instead of apologizing, I sighed and leaned my head against his shoulder.

"Was that the romance I was promised?"

He laughed, "That and the mountain of presents downstairs that have your name on them."

"I saw that. Don't you think two was enough?" I asked.

His fingers threaded into my hair, and he kissed my neck, "Nothing will ever be enough."

11

What I wanted first thing in the morning was dick. Unfortunately, I was given tea, orange juice, and a very filling breakfast instead. I opened my mouth to complain, but Azreal shot me such a deadly glare that I immediately stopped talking and returned to my plate.

It wasn't how I'd remembered it. Sure, he'd made me come like a faucet before, but this was different. As I watched his fingers grip the fork and bring the food to his lips, all I could think of was riding his face. Bouncing so hard on his dick that it snapped off and stayed inside me forever.

"The answer is still no," he said, without looking at me.

"What?" I pretended I had no idea what he was talking about as I took a bite of toast.

"That 'fuck me' pout you've given me for the last twenty minutes." I went to interject, but he cut me off, "No. Eat, Eden."

Grumbling, I skewered my tomato and took a bite of it off my fork. Az quirked an eyebrow at me as the juice dripped off my chin. I caught the liquid with my finger before shoving it into my mouth. Instead of commenting, he went back to his own plate. But I could see a very impressive tent is his sweats. I guess he wasn't immune to my charms after all...

Twenty minutes later, I was being brought down to the ground floor. The woman I'd seen a grand total of one time walked past us to go collect our dishes. Az nodded politely at her as I gave her a brilliant smile.

"Thank you, lady, that I can't know the name of because Lord Azreal is afraid I'm going to run screaming from him."

Az's hand gripped mine tighter as the woman gave a belly laugh.

"I'm called Janet, dear," she replied, shooting me a wink.

Az shot her a look and she charged up the rest of the stairs as he dragged me down.

"That was rude. I want to thank Janet," I said.

"She gets a paycheck," he said, gruffly.

"Still," I grumbled, tugging fruitlessly at his grip as he led me to the Christmas tree in the foyer. It was still swallowing the whole room. The mound of gifts was more overwhelming than it had been when I didn't know they were all mine.

"Sit," he ordered, giving me the same frustrated glance he'd given Janet.

"I'm not a dog, my lord," I huffed out with a smile. He took two steps at a time, grabbing handfuls of my ass, bringing me flush against him. A thick, hot erection laid between us, and I smiled innocently up at him, glad that all my teasing was having such an effect on him.

"Eden," he snapped.

My eyes met his, and I saw the fire blazing in them. He was clearly trying to do something cute with the presents under the tree, and I was ruining it. I smirked at him and felt the erection he was determined to ignore.

"Yes," I replied, my voice saccharine sweet. My palm moved as my fingers gripped his balls.

"You make it so hard—"

"I know."

"—to focus," he hissed, as his hand pulled mine tight and moved against him for a moment before his mouth surged forward, catching me off guard.

The kiss was bruising. Something about it felt like he was punishing himself as much as me. He ravaged my mouth, biting my lips so hard that I was surprised that I wasn't tasting blood. My pussy was so soaked by the time he pulled away that I was ready to fuck him right there.

"Sit," he ordered again.

This time I listened. I knew I wasn't the only one affected by what was wedged between us and if I pushed too hard, I wasn't going to get whatever present he was handing me or that delicious dick that I'd spent the early hours of the morning coming all over.

He reached under the tree and looked at a few different gifts until he found the one that he was looking for. I watched with bated breath, like a kid, well, like, a kid on Christmas morning. He took the first step up the stairs and handed it to me.

It was a large box, but it wasn't really heavy. I wanted to shake it, but I resisted the urge. It was dated a few days ago. I traced his handwriting scrawled across the blue snowflake wrapping paper. It surprised me that he'd done such a meticulous job wrapping, but it probably shouldn't have. Everything about him was precise. When I looked up at him, he was watching me, waiting.

"Go on," he encouraged.

My fingers slipped under the tape and I tore up, revealing a black box. Az balled up the paper as I shook off the lid. There was a framed piece of paper inside. When I pulled it out, I saw it was a map of the United States. I was confused until I looked at the map's annotations.

Areas were highlighted with dates and city names. It was everywhere I'd been in the last two years. When I got back to America, I couldn't find the right fit. I'd gone from state to state, trying to settle down, but nothing felt right. My fingers traced a line from New York to Oregon before moving down to Arizona.

He'd been watching me the whole time.

My gaze found New York again. "How'd you get Howie to give me the money if their heirlooms were fake?" I asked, not looking away from the map.

"Money," was all he replied.

My fingers found the short time I'd spent in Texas. There was an asterisk next to the date. Az sat behind me on the stairs, his thighs bracketing my sides.

"I did see you, didn't I?" I asked.

I thought I was crazy. The airport was busy, and I was on my way out after a little tiny grift on this executive whose grandfather had tricked some natives out of their land. My carry-on had a beautiful Manet rolled up inside, and I knew at least three fences that would pay top dollar for it. I was looking at my phone when I felt someone's attention on me. It was the middle of summer, and the airport was teeming with folks, but I could see him.

Az was standing on the second floor, looking right at me as I sat by my gate. My throat tightened, and it felt like something was squeezing my chest. I moved my phone to take a picture and zoom in. There was no way. The airport was tiny and domestic, he wouldn't be there. When I pointed my camera at him, he was gone. I stood, looking around, but I didn't see him or anyone who looked like him.

"I'd needed to see you," he replied. His finger brushed across Minnesota. "I was there too."

"I mean, I wasn't going to pass up the chance to see—"

"Paisley Park," we said at the same time. He smiled at me and my heart fluttered. Full-on fluttered, like some animal was trapped in my chest, and was looking to escape.

"This was hanging in my office. Seeing where you were made me feel like I wasn't crawling out of my skin," he brought his nose to my neck and I shuddered. "I don't think I can let you go again."

I turned to tell him thank you, but instead of talking, my mouth found his as I crawled into his lap and erased the space between us. His hands found my face, turning my face to gently caress my mouth with his. My tongue tried to pull harder at his tongue, but he was determined to slowly and methodically kiss me until I was dripping. I had my hands under his turtleneck when a gentle throat clearing had me pulling away from him. Somehow, I'd ended up stretched out on top of him, and we were splayed across the stairs.

"Apologies," Janet said, her cheeks red as she winked at me. "I'd love to move past you before I see my Lord's cock."

"For fuck's sake," Az growled as he sat up. I tried to move off his lap, but he held me tight against his erection.

"Sorry, Janet," I muttered, feeling the heat in my own cheeks as my core twinged. The feeling of his dick pressed right where I wanted him was making me half-feral and I had to calm down.

"I'll nip off to the kitchen, and you won't see me for the rest of the day," she said, passing by us. Pausing at the landing of the stairs, she turned around. "Any requests for dinner?"

Az made a noise of frustration as I answered, "Maybe a curry?"

"There's a lovely shop down the road," her grin was so wide, I was sure her face was going to split.

"Do they do a good butter chicken?" I asked, as Az's grip on my waist became painful. I shifted and he quietly groaned.

"They do! Roti? Or naan?"

"I will give you five grand to leave," Az ground out.

"Janet, I think you should hold out for more. At least ten thousand quid. He can afford—" I hollered as he planted his feet and used the banister to lift us both from the stairs. I grabbed his neck as he turned and carried me up the stairs.

"Bye, Janet." I called as we moved. He made it to the second floor and took me right into the room closest to us. Everything was sheathed in dust covers.

"You better still be giving—"

He plunged his fingers into me and I cried out in surprise. Grabbing the edge of my pants, he yanked them before freeing his dick and thrusting up into me. I grabbed at his shoulders as he grabbed my ass and pulled back, finding his home, deep inside me.

The angle was insane. I stood up on my tippy-toes as my wrists were yanked behind my ass cheeks as he moved in and out of me. The pace was aggressive as each stroke brought him flush against my clit. Our moans and groans mixed with the sounds of wet flesh slapping. The sounds were obscene and made my flesh burn even hotter.

My fierce orgasm set off his. I greedily pulled him in and fought against his hold as I came apart, and he muffled his shout in my neck. We stayed connected as he released my wrists and I brought my lips to his. We sat, open-mouthed, trying to get our bearings. My tongue crept out to trace his lower lip.

"You were saying about my 'fuck me' pout," I said. He pumped into me, softening, but still hard enough to send electric pleasure straight through me.

"Braggart," he said as I moaned.

"Pushover," I replied, laughing as he nipped my lip before kissing me and pulling himself free.

My cum was drenching my thighs and I could feel his beginning to drip from my pussy lips. Breaking free, he grabbed my hair and exposed my neck to his kisses and bites.

"Glutton," he licked a trail to my ear. "You're going to bleed me dry." He brought his fingers back to my clit, circling slowly and making my legs shake.

"We'll bleed out together," I moaned, moving my hips against his hand.

I was well-sated by the time we made it out of the room. We'd spent hours spread across the draped furniture, and it was a good thing it was covered. I just hoped Janet didn't hear me screaming as I squirted in Az's mouth and begged for every inch of his glorious dick. That man was turning me inside out and I was more than happy to fall apart in his arms.

12

December 17th, 2024

Az was on his laptop on the couch next to me as I read and nursed my deliciously sore ladybits. We'd spent practically all of yesterday fucking and rediscovering each other's bodies. I didn't think I'd ever been so spent before. But, even though I was worn-out, I knew that if he so much as breathed in my direction, I'd be soaked in seconds, ready for whatever he had to offer.

He'd been typing on his computer ever since we'd found our way in here after lunch. His scent was still on my skin, but if I leaned my head back, I got just enough distance from it to focus. That's why I'd found a book that I knew I could fall into to distract me. And so far it was working. But I could see him eyeing me out of the corner of my eye. He put his laptop to the side and tapped the couch.

"Come here," he said low.

"Az, I'm trying to read, not get pussy juice all over your velvet couch."

Shaking his head, he grabbed my waist and hauled me to him. I yelped in protest, but let him hold me in place. I liked it when he surrounded me like this. When he was sure I wasn't going to move, he let my waist go to grab his laptop.

He plucked the book from my hands and placed the open laptop on my thighs. The program I'd seen before was up. Navigating off the screen, he pulled up the pub and double-clicked. A series of windows popped open from social media sites. Double-clicking one opened a post on a message board that detailed a weird night that someone had while out. The folks in the chat were urging her to go to the hospital and get tested.

The next one was a video where the woman was talking about testing positive for a series of STIs after going to a bar while visiting friends. Each story was more horrifying than the next. By the time we got to missing person posts, I wanted more than a man's hands in a basket. I wanted them all to bleed.

After the sixth post, the laptop closed, and I was practically vibrating.

"How do you stop the rage from taking over?" I asked, closing my eyes, trying to purge my mind of the thoughts.

"I don't. I'm not good. A good man wouldn't do what I do. But I don't need to be good, Eden, I need to be effective. Every crime has a weight, and that weight can't continue to be carried by the innocent. So, I channel my fury into this." His hands tapped the laptop and my fingers found his and squeezed tight before letting go.

"This is never going to end, is it?" I asked, leaning my head against his shoulder.

"I'm not trying to fix the world, Eden. Just my corner of it," his thumbs kneaded at my muscles and I dropped my head, giving him better access. After a few minutes, all the rage was pulled from me by his talented hands. Hands that had been butchering people for decades.

Silence sat between us as I let him ease the tension from my body. But that dark part of my brain, the one that he'd awakened that night he'd carved that man like a roast turkey. That part wanted blood. It wanted vengeance for all these people who'd been harmed. For all of those that had disappeared across the country.

"What if I think they deserve to suffer? Does that make me just as broken as you?" I whispered the words so low I could barely hear them. I couldn't believe that I was admitting it out loud, that I was acknowledging the bloodlust simmering in my veins.

"That makes you honest," Az said into my ear as his hands circled my chest to give me a tight hug I didn't realize I needed.

"I think I'm going to enjoy this." My stomach dropped as I said my worst fear aloud.

"And that, princess, is what makes you free," he replied, kissing my cheek. "Let's go get them."

We were in the car and headed to Andover. The twins were Luc and Leo, and they owned a letting agency that operated in Hampshire, and, just our luck, they were hosting an open house. I'd told Az that coming at the very end gave us the opportunity to catch them alone instead of getting them individually at their homes. He'd looked at me like I was crazy, but he agreed and seemed to be okay with me making a few decisions.

As the car rolled to a stop in front of the house, I unbuckled my seat belt and watched Az as he eyed me. After everything I'd read, I was itching to get my hands on these men. One of them was an ex-con, and he'd apparently not learned that assault was bad because his convictions hadn't stopped him. He'd just learned to be better at it.

"Be careful, Eden," Az said as I opened the car door.

"Of course," I said. "Give me five and then come in?" I didn't wait for an answer as I closed the door and walked up the pathway. I had a plan. And in order for it to work, Azreal had to lay back and let me work.

I shook my curls out and unzipped my coat. By the time I came through the door, I was giving my best breathless, ditzy performance.

"Hi, oh my God, am I too late? I'm too late, aren't I?" I punched up the Valley Girl, California accent.

The twins were in the middle of shutting off the lights and I gave them a pout.

"Oh. Shit. I'm so sorry. I just love this location, and I was really hoping to move further from London," I babbled, giving them time to take the bait. They were identical, and one of them was clearly interested in my tits. He gave his brother a nod.

"Not at all, love. Let me take your coat," his brother reluctantly said, grabbing my jacket.

"Oh, yes! Thank you so much. You are both lifesavers. Most folks would've been long gone!" I laid it on thick as I passed it over and watched as the lecherous twin waved his hand toward the hallway.

His smile was greasy, and I didn't like the way he had me walk ahead of him, but I knew he would be getting his comeuppance, so I let him believe that he was in control. A hand hit my lower back, and I resisted the temptation to shove him away.

"Is the neighborhood quiet?" I said, leading us to the bedroom furthest from the living room.

"Very," he said, close enough to my ear that I wanted to puke. "Are you moving alone?"

I suppressed a shiver and leaned in to his hand. "Yep, just me. What about you, you got anyone special?"

He chuckled behind me and pushed me into the room, his hands roughly grabbing my hip. "Is that an invitation?" he asked. I put my hand in my jean pocket and peeled the back off the adhesive before slapping it on to his meaty neck.

"Nope," I smiled.

He was confused for a second, "I'm—" his words slurred as his eyes rolled back, and he hit the ground. Hard. I looked down the hallway and his brother hadn't heard him fall. Good. The patch took longer on him than it did on me, but it worked. I peeled the adhesive off the second one and took a bracing breath into my belly before I yelled.

"Are you okay? Oh my god! Help. Help." I leaned down and started to shake his unconscious form.

"What's wrong?" A bellow came from down the hall, and his brother charged in, wide-eyed as he leaned down. "Call 999!" he yelled.

"He rubbed at his arm," I said, eyeing his thick sweater and jacket. Shit.

"His arm?" He shook his brother and went to check his pulse. I leaned forward to paste the patch to the small patch of skin I could see when he jerked back and saw it in my hand and snatched my wrist, holding it in a crushing grip.

"What the fuck? What did you do to my brother?" he bellowed.

"Nothing, it's—"

He yanked my arm down as he looked at his brother's neck, spotting the patch. When his fingers caught the edge of the adhesive, I brought my knee up to his face. His grip loosened enough for me to yank my wrist away and crawl across the room.

His hand grabbed my ankle, and I kicked at his face with my booted foot, watching as he fell back. I managed to stand and got to the hallway before I was tossed against the wall. Fingers gripped at my neck, but I smiled wide and toothy.

"What the fuck are you smiling at, bitch?" His words came with spittle flying from his mouth, and I winced.

"First, say it, don't spray it. Wait, is that a saying here too?"

He smacked my head against the wall and my ears started to ring.

"Eden." The yell came from the door as his fingers started to loosen, and he staggered back, looking at the back of his hand with the adhesive square firmly placed against his skin. He swayed for a second before falling, cracking his head against the wall.

Adjusting my shirt and hair, I put my hands on my hips and puffed out my chest.

"She don't need no man, she's got it on her own. She's Poison Eden!" I sang. I made eye contact with Az and I couldn't for the life of me decipher the look on his face. After a second, I brought my arms back down.

"No congratulations or anything? Damn. Tough crowd," I mumbled, walking to the bedroom.

13

December 18th, 2024

"You did a remarkable job," Az said, dipping his spoon into his soft-boiled egg.

This conversation was a wonderful distraction from the raw ass food he was shoving in his mouth. Az hadn't said anything to me last night as he emptied their pockets and hefted both men into the trunk of the SUV. When we tied them down, he just instructed me on the knots and didn't say much more. We left the men trussed up and taped to hell in their cell, closing and locking the heavy door behind us.

When we went upstairs, he gave me a very polite peck on the cheek at my door before going to his own room and closing the door. All the adrenaline coursing through me had faded, and I was annoyed. I'd done what I said I would, why was he acting like I fucked it up?

It wasn't the first time he'd acted like I'd thrown off his whole routine. When I stopped that woman from getting drugged, he'd looked at me like I was crazy, but it had nothing to do with the woman. And suddenly, we were right back to the beginning. For someone who wanted desperately to show me this side of his life, he was acting like I was a barrier and not someone who could help him.

Crossing my arms in front of me, I shoved my oatmeal across the table. "But," I said, eyeing him as he put his spoon down. Thank god, the jiggling runny egg on his spoon was icky.

"You didn't see what I saw," he said.

"I had it handled," I replied. And I did. I mean, he got a few good licks, but I was able to get the patch on him before he could actually hurt me.

"Allowing you to go in on your own was a mistake." His eyes fell to the bruise on my wrist, and I rolled my eyes. We'd agreed to it. They would've been instantly on guard if he'd come in with me. They didn't expect a big booty bitch to get the drop on them, and it showed. Definitely should've thought about the winter aspect of it all, though. You can't get a patch of skin if they're covered head to toe. Lesson learned.

"I'm fine. It's just a bruise or two." I shrugged, watching as he narrowed his eyes. "And we have them now. So we're good," I said. I didn't care what weird faces he made, I was happy with myself. "I'm going to take my oatmeal to the library until you can find the words to say what you need to." I stood, grabbing my food and walking out of the sunroom.

Az didn't stop me.

The sun was starting to set, and I'd just gotten up to turn on the lights. Everything about this library was a dream. Sure, it was blood money that built and furnished it, but it cracked me up that I was sitting, feet up, ass half out, in a library built on slavery money.

Az didn't speak to it much, but I knew his father's family legacy bothered him. If his ancestors knew their sole living heir was going to look straight from the Motherland, they probably would've killed themselves.

Hell, they were most likely trying to break through the veil as they saw two brown folks fucking all over the mansion. Laughing, I lifted my middle finger, praying they were stuck watching what had become of their legacy. I'm sure the devil thought it was the best kind of torture.

"I wasn't expecting a warm welcome, but I can't help but hope that's not for me," Az said from the doorway.

Laying on the couch cushion with my legs up on the arm, I stared at his upside-down face. "Nope. But if you're not coming in here to use your words, it just might be."

"Eden." He took a deep breath and placed his hands behind his back. Ruh roh. That was never a good sign. "I love you. And while I do want you to be with me in this, I didn't expect to feel so... gutted every time you put yourself in harm's way. I just need to adjust. You've done nothing wrong."

My mouth was open as I stared at him. The book fell into my face and I barely even felt the impact. I mean, I knew that he cared about me. But to hear that he was fighting his urge to keep me safe and that turned him into a monosyllabic dickhead. It wasn't at all what I was expecting.

"Come to dinner," he held out his hand to me as I stared up at him. "Or you can give me the two-finger salute, and *then* you can come to dinner." That dazzling smile was back, and my brain felt like it was starting to short-circuit.

"I need a minute," I muttered.

He scrunched up his face, confused. "A minute, for?" Bless his heart.

Clearing my throat, I gently moved my legs to the floor and sat upright. "Well, you just said something I've never heard you say," I spoke slowly, wondering if he was having a stroke or if it was me.

"The last time we tried to do romance, you passed out. I figured blunt was better this go around," he said, giving me a placating look.

"That doesn't mean—"

"We can have this discussion upstairs. You haven't eaten since breakfast."

"I—How did you? Never mind. You can't just—"

He stepped forward, looking down at me with a raised eyebrow.

"Fine. I'm getting up. I know you're stronger than you look," I grumbled.

He took my hand, and we walked upstairs to the sunroom where dinner was laid out on the small table. Az pulled out my chair and I sat, staring off into space as he piled my plate with spaghetti, veggies, and placed a piece of flatbread on the small plate beside mine. As he filled his own plate, he started to talk.

"Maybe we can go to the tapas place in Covent Garden, there's a show at the Coward that seems good." I opened my mouth to speak, and he cut me off. "Take your minute. Eat. We'll talk when you're through." He gave me a stern look and I lifted my fork and skewered a piece of broccoli, bringing it to my mouth. "I haven't been able to stop loving you these last two years." I took a quick breath in as he said it again, pieces of the floret bounced along my windpipe. Az pushed the water toward me and kept talking, "That's not going to change in the next twenty minutes."

Giving him a glare of my own, I sipped the water as my throat burned.

"If you're not feeling tapas, we can always eat here. Or we can do dim sum."

I'd never seen Azreal babble, but he was doing a marvelous job of it. I watched as he moved his hands, animatedly, while I swirled spaghetti around my fork and started to fill my belly. It was good, but I couldn't really taste it, I was trying to get my brain to compute.

Thankfully, his talking gave me the space I needed to think. I'd come into this as a way of fucking him out of my system, but all I'd done was spend the whole time getting hooked on him while finding a connection so unique that I wondered if I would ever be able to feel this comfortable again.

And, even if that was even possible, I didn't want it with anyone else, I wanted it with the man currently ranking all the plays he'd seen since I was gone and talking about each one that I would enjoy and how we would see them when they came back to the city. All of this was normal. Every inch of it. I hadn't had normal in such a long time, I didn't know what it looked like.

Maybe this was it.

When I put down my fork, he was watching me, his plate half full because he'd spent more time talking than eating. He was looking for some kind of sign that I was ready to talk, and I nodded to him.

"I watched over you, waiting for you to come back to me. Of course, I'm in love with you, Eden. And you're in love with me." He took a few more bites, unbothered by the alarmed noises I was making. "You'll say it when

you're ready. Until then, we can go back to the library."
He stood and leaned toward me. "I'm sensing you need
more quiet time than you thought.

I let him escort me back to the library. Maybe I did
love him? I mean, we'd kidnapped two men, bound and
gagged them downstairs, and were planning to pass
judgment on them for the fucked up shit they'd been
doing for years. This was the most fun I'd had in my
entire life. And I wanted it to last well beyond Christmas.

Shit.

14

The rubber gloves were thick, and the Wellington boots felt like too much, but Az told me I needed them. He was behind me, tightening a rubber apron to my waist. I marveled at the cleanliness of the room that had just days ago been showered in blood. Part of me was curious how his cleaning system worked, how he disposed of the offenders, but this wasn't the time for fifty-eleven questions—we had plans.

The thrum of anticipation had my skin tingling, and I was ready to go inside to truly meet the men responsible for the pain and suffering of so many women. Az's face found his favorite spot in the back of my neck, and he took a moment, breathing me in. It was quickly becoming my favorite thing.

"Ready, princess?" he asked.

"Yes, my lord," I replied with a nod.

He reached out, tracing the shell of my ear down to my jaw. "You make me so hard when you say that," he whispered.

It took everything in me not to purr like a cat. Touch was one of Az's love languages. Touch had never been something that I really wanted, but this was different. It wasn't an act put on to lull someone into a false sense of security. Nor was it some quickie hand job with a finger up the booty that put my mark to sleep so I could ransack his safe.

It was real.

"What are you smiling at?" Az asked as he tied his apron behind his back.

"You don't wanna know," I replied, laughing. He gave me a look and paused, slapping his rubber gloves against his hand. "Okay, I was thinking about how hard men sleep after you stick a finger up their poop chute."

He tilted his head. There wasn't alarm in his gaze, but maybe I was sensing a little... fascination? "You've never put your finger up my—"

"No," I confirmed. "You'd know if I did," I laughed, but he didn't.

"Is that something you... like to do?" he asked.

"I mean, if you like it?" I shrugged. Oh, he was definitely fascinated.

He looked deep in thought as he pulled on his gloves. "I don't think I would?"

I smirked, shaking my head. That sounded like a maybe to me, but it wasn't the time for that particular conversation. "Well, if you're ever curious." My fingers waggled in his face and he stared at them for a moment, not saying a word.

Stepping back, he grabbed a leather case from his work-bench and walked over to the door. There was a slot at eye level that he flipped open. When he was sure that things were as we left them, he swung the door open.

Muffled cursing met us as we walked in. The walls were also stone and there were drains along the floor that led left and right. It hadn't been twenty-four hours, but the stench of piss was wafting through the room. Thankfully, they hadn't shitted on themselves. But, considering what the plan was, that might change.

Even in the light of the room, they looked practically the same. Broad shoulders, clean-shaven, with angry brown eyes and sandy brown hair. Each chair was bolted to the ground and the tape and rope job had held firmly.

They were right where we'd left them, even if the room did smell like rancid peepee and fear.

Fear was good. That was exactly what I wanted them to feel.

"Luc and Leo Grayson. Or is it Leo and Luc. No matter, we'll get to that," Az had the same tone he'd adopted the last time we were down here, and it sent a little thrill through me. I was starting to love watching this man work.

The men were screaming behind their gags and glaring at us. Az dropped the leather medicine bag by his feet. He gave the men a little shush as he unzipped it and looked through it, cataloging the instruments that I couldn't quite see before standing upright.

"Luc has been convicted of sexual assault, did you know that, princess?"

"I did, didn't he drug her with something?" I asked, crossing my hands across my chest as he pulled out two prefilled misters. He handed me one, and I watched as he sprayed the mist up one brother's nose before looking back at me.

My hands tightened on it as I looked at the angry face of the man in front of me. I thought about what he had coming, and I didn't even hesitate. I leaned forward, grabbing and holding his chin to spray up and into his nostril. As he yanked free of my hold, I smiled at him. This was the one I'd fought in the hallway, I was sure of it.

I don't know what I'd expected as I stood in front of him. Maybe I thought I would be afraid, or I'd feel something shift and break in me. But everything at that moment felt right. I was helping to dole out the justice that some in our society never received, and it felt—good.

"It's just GHB. I believe that is the preferred method," Az said, pulling the mister from my hand and throwing it towards the corner.

Grabbing the brother's jaw, I made sure he was looking at me as I spoke. "So Luc was caught before, what, eight years ago? But he never stopped raping women, did he?"

Az looked at me, his eyes sharp. "Which one do you reckon is Luc?"

I looked between them and neither seemed to want to fess up. "Come on, Luc, be honest," my voice was saccharine. The one in front of Az was blinking—a lot. "I think you're Luc," I said. Az grabbed a pair of scissors from the bag and held them out to me. "We're going to have a little chat, Luc. You'll admit what you've done.

Then, your brother will admit what he's done. And then you'll be able to go on home. Okay?"

He nodded vigorously, and I cut a little of the tape and yanked it free of his mouth. The skin blistered and bled, but he didn't yell or beg. He stayed silent, waiting. "What was the number you had so far, my lord?"

"Thirty-eight," Az replied.

I didn't startle, but I was surprised. That's what he'd been doing all day. Finding more victims. Almost forty women had been raped by these men. Castration was too easy for them. The suffering wasn't immense enough. I took a big breath as I watched the fear in the man's eyes.

"Alright, Luc. We believe that you and your brother have assaulted over thirty-eight women. What are you thinking? Higher? Lower?"

Luc stammered, "I don't—higher?"

I nodded and patted his leg. "That's good. Honesty is good. Some of the women from that pub disappeared. Do you know anything about that?"

Leo was vigorously shaking his head in my peripheral, but I grabbed Luc's face and made sure I had his attention.

"What?" His eyes darted back and forth, but I tutted in disappointment.

"We were doing the honesty thing. Remember?" I kept my tone light but increased my grip on his jaw.

"I-I-I'd check their phones. If we thought no one would miss them, we'd call a guy."

Leo was screaming and grumbling in his chair. Confessing to rape was fine, but snitching was clearly outside his bounds of comfort. Az walked over and punched the fuck out of him. Luc's eyes got wide as they looked from Az to me. Leo's muffled groans replaced his protests, and I brought the conversation back to where we were.

"Hey, hey. Luc. Focus. We just want a name. That's all."

"You're going to kill us," he wailed, tears filling his eyes.

"Us? No. My lord, are we going to kill these gentlemen?" I asked, catching Az's eyes.

"Not as long as they're honest," Az replied.

I patted Luc's leg. "See, scout's honor. You're not going to remember any of this with that drug in your system. That's how you've been able to get away with all this, right? Just give us a name."

There was a deep pause as he looked between the three of us. His brother was shaking his head, but Luc was determined. He looked right at me and said, "Renault Russo."

"Thank you, that was so kind of you," I stood up straight and patted his shoulder. Now was the part that I was most looking forward to. When Az mentioned his judgment, he gave me a moment to opt-out. But I needed to see this through. And these fucking jerks deserved every inch of pain coming to them.

"Please, let us go!" Luc squealed.

"Would you say you've learned your lesson?" I asked, my tone mocking.

"Yes, yes. Please," he begged.

"You promise?" I asked.

"I promise," he swore.

"I believe you." A deep sense of satisfaction filled me as I watched the tears filling his eyes spill over his cheeks. And the momentary relief of him thinking he was free to go fed my rage. "Because he's going to chop your dick off."

"No. No. Why? No, no, please, no, oh my god." Luc's words were barely coherent under the sobbing.

"Castration is quite easy, princess. Don't you think it's too easy?" Az asked.

I looked at him, confused. "I'm curious to hear your suggestions."

"Please, don't please, I swear I'll—" I grabbed the tape from the bag and placed a fresh piece across his face.

"Shh, mommy and daddy are judging," I said, pinching his cheek.

"Losing something is difficult, but that false hope that it might work again. It could be the perfect reminder that they've been harmed and will never be whole again. I think it's fitting. Especially since one of these bastards likes to inflict pain."

He was right. Losing it all together was easier than having a useless glob of meat hanging between their legs. I tilted my head in thought before I nodded. "Okay. Over forty lives have been irrevocably changed. That sounds like a judgment that fits the crime. I agree."

Az gave me a nod and kissed my forehead, "Check their restraints for me, my love?"

I jumped and gave him a look that told him I needed him to stop saying that. He just winked at me as he grabbed a few things out of his bag. Shaking my head, I pulled at their binds. Their yanking and pulling was becoming uncoordinated. The GHB was kicking in.

A part of me wanted them to remember this. They deserved the horror of watching someone taking something from them. They deserved to watch as their lives were permanently altered in the same way that they demolished the lives of others.

Breathing into my diaphragm, I closed my eyes and tried to leash my anger. The first breath wasn't good enough, so I took two more. When I opened my eyes, Az watched me, his eyes full of understanding. He was giving me a moment to adjust.

Rage wasn't the goal—balance was. They needed to carry the weight their victims already were.

We were so connected at that moment, it was like I was seeing him for the first time. It would be easy to feed into all the emotions threatening to explode from my chest. A startling thought piped up—this was the same man. His face was the same. His smile was the same. The way he walked and talked was all the same. This was the same man and I was *absolutely* in love with him. I'd never stopped loving him. Blinking, I brought my attention back to the moment we were in because we had a job to do.

I nodded to Az. I was ready.

"Now," Az said as he sliced open Luc's pants and boxers before lifting his shriveled dick into his gloved hand, "There's a nerve here that controls movement." Luc's balls retracted as he tried and failed to pull away from Az. "Thank you, that helps me see where I'm going. I slice here," Az spoke as he ran the scalpel smoothly up the base, blood squirted out and Luc screamed and screamed, but Az kept steady pressure moving his scalpel past the skin and into the muscle.

Blood plopped heavily against the floor and I could hear it hitting the stone as the screaming faded to pained grunts. I watched as it soaked through his pants and splashed up to hit the apron that Az was wearing. It was coating everything and as Az continued to carve into him, the pool grew bigger.

"It's this thick vein. And this nerve here," Az said, making sawing motions, and a blood geyser squirted against his chest. Luc's eyes rolled back as he passed out, but Azreal continued his ministrations, looking through the blood to the veins he was dissecting.

"Should I get the salts?" I asked, my gaze hypnotized by the sight.

"No. I'm almost done. Just one final detail."

He reached his bloody hand into his case and sprayed the contents of a glass syringe on to the wound and then all over the shaft and head. The liquid sizzled across the skin, blistering and burning straight through to the muscle.

"Just a little longer. Wouldn't want the lad to lose it," he said, taking a step back. After a few more seconds, he grabbed a box of baking soda and coated the mauled dick, stopping the chemical burns.

Az turned to me. Adrenaline had blown out his pupils. The stench of blood and fear didn't phase him. If anything, it made him enjoy it. And I enjoyed watching him. I was a little queasy. But something in me was blessed to be here, watching on behalf of the victims that weren't. And nothing was going to stop me from seeing this through.

I turned to see Leo, wide-eyed and making noises that could only be him vomiting into his mouth and swallowing. Az moved his bag over as Leo's head lolled. When Az got to work on Leo, I noticed his pain tolerance was much higher. Instead of screaming, he was cursing beneath the tape as silent tears fell from his eyes.

"Is that what some of the women did when you raped them? Silent tears? A stiff upper lip?" I asked. I leaned close, thick crimson liquid smacking against my own apron as Az severed veins and carved into muscles. His angry eyes met mine and I tilted my head, knowing that I was right.

"You should be lucky you're getting away with your life," I whispered before grabbing his face. "I'm going to track down each and every victim. And when I find the ones you sold, I'll be back. And it won't be a body part that you lose."

Leo passed out as Az dug into his vein, and it shot blood everywhere. When the acid finally hit his skin, I took a step back. I was breathing hard as I marveled at the sheer amount of blood soaking the floor. Az applied the baking soda and turned to me. He was dripping crimson. A hand reached out to grab me, but he rethought his decision, letting his arm fall back to his side.

"Are you okay?" he asked, watching me for any signs that I was ready to flee.

"Yeah, I'm good," I said, removing the heavy gloves from my hands, angrily.

A breath I didn't see him holding released in a whoosh, and the tension left his shoulders. He looked down at himself and then at me.

"I'll box them up and take them back where we found them. Shouldn't take me more than an hour." He pointed at the back door we'd brought them both through.

"Okay. I'll head upstairs," I said, my fingers finding the knot for the apron behind my neck.

"My quarters. Robert lit the fireplace for you, he's laundering your—"

"There's a fireplace in your room?!" I screeched. He raised his eyebrow. "I've been an entire frosted-titty snowman, and you have a fireplace in your room?"

"You could have—"

"Nah, I'm taking your room, you can sleep somewhere else. I can't believe you let my toes turn into icicles. I'm going on strike. No pussy for you!" I said, throwing down the apron and gloves.

"You could have asked," he said, his smile placating.

I glared at him and I pulled the Wellies from my feet, "I didn't think I had to ask not to freeze to death, Az! Basic human decency!"

He stepped closer, his voice a low rumble. "You want my room? Take it." His smirk deepened. "But don't think I won't join you. It's my bed, after all."

I huffed, walking away. "Try it, I'll smother you with one of your posh pillows."

His laugh followed me all the way out of the wine cellar. I felt the buzz of adrenaline start to fade as I showered, brushed my teeth, and floated through Az's warm bedroom. Even though it was cozy as shit, I couldn't find sleep. So, I laid there and stared out at the dark hills in the distance.

I should have been appalled. My soul should have felt soiled and black. I'd just stolen the manhood of two men. I'd watched another lose his hands. And the disembowelment... But that's not what was living in my thoughts. It was images of murdered women, photos from rape kits, and tales of missing loved ones.

What we'd just done helped stop another forty women from being hurt, but it wasn't going to do much for those who had already been victimized. Now I saw why Az had his strict system. If I'd let my emotions cloud my judgement, I could've justified killing them. But death wasn't the equalizer those men needed. They needed to suffer.

Later that night, when Az snuggled up next to me, I was still grumpy, but I was so cozy and warm that I didn't even complain when he slipped beneath the covers. He smelled like soap and minty toothpaste.

"I didn't think you'd be awake," he whispered, kissing my neck.

"I'm not," I replied, putting my face further into the pillow.

"Hmm, so about that strike." He was using that bass-y voice that made my toes curl. But I wasn't that easy.

"Still going," I said.

"I had the fire started for you." He gave a fake whine, trying to bargain.

"Robert started the fire. Maybe I'll give him some pussy if he's not busy," I muttered, cuddling into his arms.

"He's currently cleaning up the dungeon, but I'm sure he has some time tomorrow," He said, laughing.

"I'll pencil him in," I yawned.

He nipped at my back. "I'm sure he'll be thrilled."

15

December 22nd, 2024

We fell into a rhythm the next few days. There were countless orgasms, but mostly we got to know each other with our masks off. I told him how much losing my mother drove me to embrace life. How I'd gone to the British Museum every week so I could feel like she was still with me. Az showed me a hammered bangle his mother had worn every day, a giant and stunning cyan chrysocolla stone at the center, and how she talked about how proud she was of him before she passed away.

I'd known that things had shifted, but I didn't realize how much. Az had an important meeting in the city that he couldn't miss. So, after he'd spent the morning worshiping every inch of my body with his tongue and his hands, he took a quick shower and ran to catch his train.

Blissed out, I found myself wandering into the kitchen an hour later to see Janet and Robert. She was always all smiles and eager to laugh, but he was the exact opposite.

"That's a very nice coat, Robert," I said.

"Thanks, ma'am," he replied.

"You do a great job," I smiled as he turned and looked uncomfortable.

"Thank you, ma'am," he answered.

I was using every tool in my arsenal to break the permanent mask on his face, and it wasn't working. Maybe I could convince Az to give him more money. That would make *me* smile if I was him. I started to say something about the way he was organizing the cabinet when Janet touched my shoulder.

"You haven't noticed," she whispered.

"Hmm?" I turned and followed her gaze. She was looking at the door and the light that had been red was now green. I couldn't remember the last time I'd even checked the doors... How long had they been unlocked?

"Go on, take a walk, dear," she said.

The first place I visited was the pond. Robert practically threw the fruit and veg at me as I walked out of the kitchen. He was a curmudgeon, but dammit, did I like a challenge. I was eager to know more about them and how they found each other, but there was plenty of time to ask those questions later.

Our deal was supposed to last another three days, but there was no way that I was leaving now. Over the last nine days, I felt like I was awake in a way I hadn't been— ever. When Az passed judgement on those people, there was no negotiation. The evidence was clear and the response, precise. It was a breath of fresh air in a world consumed by unfairness.

My thoughts drifted to the reservation in Oklahoma, where I'd left the money I'd gotten for the Manet. The money wouldn't fix what was broken, but it was a way for them to get some kind of restitution straight from those who benefited the most from the crimes done. That was all we could do. Tip the scales a little and hoped that it helped those who'd been decimated.

I'd chosen Az, not because he was guilty, but because of his father's lineage. It was a legacy that had been built on hate. Sir Arnold King was too old to serve in World War II, so he'd spent his time and energy at the British Eugenics Institute. There he reimagined what the future of his country could look like if resources were pulled from communities of color in favor of the 'pure blood' of the aristocracy. For him, eugenics wasn't just science—it was a moral duty that ensured the 'best' people inherited the future, no matter the human cost.

When I found his name on the roster and saw how privileged Az was living, I needed to do something. He seemed like an easy target, so I found what I could out about him and his family and the gold they'd been given over a hundred years ago as a thank-you from the Crown. They'd never spent it, and it had only been seen once in a museum.

As I found myself surrounded by geese, I threw fruit at them. The swans seemed nice enough, but the way they charged me caused my tactics to change. I went from tossing handfuls of fruit into their little crowd to emptying the pot and running right for the pond. When they saw the bowl was empty, they started to pick at what I'd dropped.

I looked up at the statue that sat in the middle of the water. The copper scales were glinting in the sunshine. I believed in that balance, too. In my own way, I was adding to balance, tipping the scales. And I found someone who was also doing his part to right wrongs.

Azreal had been put in a precarious position: born into a racist aristocracy, raised by a man who could barely stand to look at his child. But he found his path through it all. And our paths were more parallel than I'd ever realized.

Hugging my coat close, I walked past the water, taking in the scent of the trees and watching as the breeze moved through the leaves. I'd found the thing that I'd never been able to when I ran back to America: a home.

16

Christmas Eve dinner was so amazing that I was going to kiss Janet full on the mouth the next time I saw her. She had made these Yorkshire puddings that I couldn't stop putting in my face. And, when I'd let it slip to her that I died for a really well-cooked prime rib, she made sure I had it. Az was smiling as he watched me pat my full belly.

"You look like you enjoyed yourself," he remarked dryly.

Rolling my eyes, I grabbed his hand and used it to rub my stomach. "All that snark, you can rub me to sleep." I leaned back and started to close my eyes.

"I have something for you."

I squinted at him as his hand rubbed higher to my chest. He pulled his chair closer and his lips found my neck, his fingers swirling around my nipple as he pulled it through my bra. Wet kisses tingled on my skin and I felt like I was floating.

"Dick?" I asked, my tone hopeful as I reached out to touch his chest. "I might need like ten minutes, so I don't barf on you, but I'm interested."

"I know you are. You can't get enough of me." His teeth found their way into my flesh and I moaned, my pussy immediately wet and ready.

"It might be the easiest job you've had yet. One orgasm, and I'm going to be in a coma," I muttered as I trailed my fingers beneath his shirt. His hands stilled mine and I frowned.

"Wait," he leaned up and gave me a kiss before he reached behind me.

"Wait?" I whined, leaning up and biting his jaw before kissing it better.

My tablet was in his hand and he passed it to me. It was open to a redacted dossier with a list of dead and their ages. The ages were all over the place, but their vacant eyes all looked the same. Some of them had needles dangling from their arms. They'd overdosed. All fifteen of them.

The police report's last update was over a year ago, and they had no leads on where the drugs had come from or who had cut them with bathroom solvent. I looked up at Az and he thumbed my cheek.

"This judgement is yours. What do you believe would be commensurate?"

I flipped back through the file, looking not only at the images of the victims, but the family statements that spoke to each of the lives that had been interrupted. The boy with the black hair that played the jazz trumpet in a ska band. The mother of four with green eyes that spiraled after having surgery on her neck. A pensioner that fought in the Falklands War and spent every Thursday playing Bingo.

Every single one of their stories was important. And the chemical this person had chosen to cut the drugs with was intentional. It was a way to increase profits and make money off folks who were already in pain. When I finally got to the rap sheet, it showed exactly what I was expecting. Charges that didn't stick. Connections to organized crime. A history of violence that started several years ago.

The man was escalating, and he would only get worse. I looked for his photo, but didn't find one. There were emails and call transcripts that connected him to some bribes of a few police officers.

He had to be stopped.

"Death," I said, never taking my eyes off the tablet.

"Are you sure?" Az asked.

"Bribes, selling narcotics, murder. Yes, absolutely."

I looked up as his hands found my face. "Are you ready to wield the hand of justice?" he asked.

"I am." And I was. I'd never been so sure of anything in my life. This is what I wanted.

"Come." He stood and held out his hand. I took it and followed him.

We walked side by side. His palm was firm in mine. The boots I had on clacked against the ground as we wound our way towards the dungeon. I steadied my breathing, feeling Az's eyes scanning me for any sign of discomfort.

When we made it to the wine cellar, he stopped and his hand came to my neck. I could tell he was worried, but instead of voicing it, he kissed my forehead and opened the door, letting me step forward first. The room smelled like bleach. Whoever was here hadn't been here long. I turned to see a familiar face.

Harden Driscoll was on his toes, hanging from a beam above his head. His wrists were crossed and taped to one another on the beam. I stepped further into the room, my footsteps echoing. His head turned towards the noise and he sneered.

"You gormless twat. Do you have any idea who you're dealing with?" He hissed, trying and failing to move his body towards me.

"Harden Driscoll, are you ready to admit your crimes?" I asked, doing nothing to conceal my voice.

"My crimes? What are you on ab— I know th— Jessa?" A booming laugh echoed through the room as I eyed the weapons organized on the table to my right. I reached over, feeling the handle of the curved blade that two years ago today had eviscerated a man.

"Your crimes: bribery, narcotics distribution, murder." My voice was steady and strong, even if my hand shook just a little.

"This isn't about my crimes. It's about the money," he said.

"Rayna Hall was drugged at a party. Only, the powder was laced with ammonia. She died. Did you do that yourself, or was it some moron who works for you?" I asked.

"Love, you think anyone does anything without my say-so." Another barking laugh filled the room.

"So, you admit your crimes?" I confirmed, my fingers gripping the handle and clutching it in my palm. My muscles were coiled tight and the air around me felt charged and heavy. My breaths were coming faster as I felt a chill crawl through me.

"I do what I want. Fuck you." He spat in my direction, but missed.

"Are you ready for your judgement?" I asked, moving slowly toward him.

"You think you can judge me? I—"

I leaned back and twisted with my hips towards his throat. The blade cut through his neck easily. As it did, blood spurted toward me, arterial spray covering my face and clothes. A gagging gurgle filled the room as blood continued to pour out from the wound and soak his clothes. Air hissed from the slash as his body started to wildly jerk against the bonds.

My fingers grabbed the cover from his eyes and I yanked his face toward me. He was panicked, and the fear had finally set in. He knew he was dying. I smelled piss as it hit the floor and turned up my nose.

"Your judgement is death. For all the harm you have caused, the only balance that can be found is you meeting your damnation," I hissed. Blood found its way out of his mouth as he coughed, choking on his blood as he tried to breathe. I watched, transfixed, until his eyes glossed over in death.

Azreal moved from the doorway, into the room. He grabbed the blade from my hand and returned it to the table. But I couldn't look away from those unseeing eyes staring back at me. The wound was still gushing blood, his heart clearly not getting the signal that the brain had given up.

When Az returned to my side, there was a wet towel in his hands, and he wiped gently at my face. My hand was shaking, and I was starting to feel lightheaded. The adrenaline that I'd felt before seemed to give way to something else.

"Come. Let's clean you up, my love."

He led me out of the room and towards the bathroom outside of the wine cellar. I started shivering as he walked over to the shower and started the water. My breath came in shallow, uneven gasps, each one catching in my throat like I'd swallowed broken glass. My legs shook so hard I could barely stand. I stumbled back, slamming into the wall, my shoulder hitting the cold tile.

My hands—fuck, my hands—felt like they weren't mine anymore. They were coated in blood. His blood. I stared at them, trying to rub it off on my jeans, but it just smeared, sinking into the fabric. It wouldn't come off.

I killed him.

The thought tore through me like a shard of ice. My chest tightened until I couldn't breathe. I pressed my fingers to my lips, but the sob ripped free anyway, raw and jagged. My knees buckled, and I slid down the wall, curling into myself.

Az was in front of me, but I couldn't bring myself to look up at him. His movements were slow, deliberate. He crouched in front of me, his dark eyes calm but focused.

"Eden, breathe," he said softly.

My body shuddered, icy chills racing up my spine. The room tilted and spun. The blood was all I could see. Az reached for my hands, wrapping his around them. His grip was steady, grounding me, but I wanted to pull away. My hands—his blood—Az didn't care. "It was necessary," he said.

I nodded. I knew that. I knew it. But that didn't stop the rampant beating of my heart in my chest or clean the blood from my skin. He saw my gaze focused on the sticky and thick crimson on my hands.

"Up," he said, pulling me to my feet.

We both walked into the shower, fully clothed, watching the blood turn the water red. He soaped the washcloth and cleaned every inch of visible skin. Once the water became a pale pink, he made quick work of the sweater and jeans I was wearing, throwing them, soaking wet, out of the shower. He then pulled off his own clothes.

Washing me again, he was thorough and quick, first me then him. Once we'd rinsed off again, he cradled me to his chest underneath the water. We sat there, feeling the cascade of hot water together in silence. My head laid against the tattoo he'd gotten since we'd been apart, and I listened as he breathed, as his heart continued it's steady and strong beat. The dizziness faded as I matched my breaths with his and focused on his strong arms around me.

His hands began running up and down the middle of my back. I pulled back and grabbed for the soap, not feeling clean enough, only for him to pull it from my hands. He moved us back from the water and he began to smooth across my neck and arms.

"I went into shock my first time, too. Your body is finding its rhythm again," he said softly, as he moved towards my chest.

I sighed, leaning into him, my tongue finding the water clinging to his skin over his tattoo. He hissed, his hands moving to my breasts and holding their weight in his hands. I dragged my lips up his neck as his dick pushed at the center of my thighs, hardening.

Humming, he pulled me against his body. I angled my face and his lips captured mine, running soapy hands across my tummy, along my curves and down to my ass. His tongue tangled with mine as he turned us back under the water. As the suds fell from my skin, I grabbed at him, feeling his stomach and waist.

There was raw power in his body. He didn't need a six-pack or crazy muscles to be fine as fuck. He was a man about his business, and he loved and cared for me. And I loved and cared for him. Leaning back, further under the spray, I looked up into his hooded eyes.

"You did so well," he said.

Az's lips trailed down my neck, slow and deliberate, his touch sending shivers across my skin. His breath was hot against my collarbone. His hands slid to my hips, firm but grounding, holding me steady. "You're so much stronger than you realize," he said.

"I don't feel like I was very strong at all," I whispered against his skin.

He pulled back just enough to meet my eyes. His gaze burned, dark and unwavering. "Because it's new. It's raw. But Eden..." His hand brushed my cheek, his thumb tracing the edge of my jaw. "You didn't crumble. You didn't look away. You found your strength and balanced the scales. That makes you extraordinary."

His fingers continued to move against my skin as I dragged my hand down to grab his length. Words were hard. I knew that Az was right. I'd done the right thing for the community, for the families, for the victims, but I felt like I was falling without a parachute. Being held by him told me just how wrong I was. He knew this world and was with me every step of the way.

"You're not afraid of what's inside you," he murmured, his lips finding mine in a slow, searching kiss. "You're afraid of what it means. But I see you. I see your kindness. Your courage. Your tenacity."

I clung to him, letting the weight of his words and his touch pull me closer. When he guided me back to the wall, his hands were reverent, exploring every inch of me as if to prove his point.

"You're mine, Eden," he whispered against my ear, his voice low and possessive. "Not because I want to control you—but because no one else will ever understand you like I do. No one else can even try."

His lips moved down my body, leaving a trail of heat in their wake. Every kiss, every touch was a promise: that I wasn't alone, that I wasn't broken, that I was more than I believed.

"Say it," he urged, his voice a husky command. "Say you're mine."

And at that moment, with the world still spinning from what I'd done, I whispered, "I'm yours."

He dropped to his knees and buried his face in my pussy. His tongue stroking through my folds to find my clit. I cried out as he nipped at it before sucking the bud into his mouth, tonguing it in patterns that I couldn't even recognize because I was already unraveling. I started to slip down the wall, and he brought my thighs to his shoulders as he continued to ravage me.

Pulling me back on his face, my lower back was in his hands as his tongue fucked in and out of me, slurping at my juices and filling the room with the sound of my guttural moans and my wet sex.

I came again, as he rubbed my slit all his mouth and tongue. My hands grabbed at the shower walls as each tremor of my orgasm rolled through me, right to Az's eager tongue. My feet were unsteady when he let me go. Instead of kissing him like I was dying too, my hands came to his dick and I fell to my knees, knocking him right against my tonsils. I dragged him all the way out before I pushed him all the way back in.

"Just like that, princess," he encouraged. And I listened, letting the saliva pool in my throat as I hummed and gagged on his dick. I found the perfect pace as I cupped his balls, squeezing them one at a time before I brought my finger up, massaging the thin layer of skin behind his balls.

The moan he let out was a mixture of surprise and delight, and I laughed, almost choking myself. I massaged him, loving the way that his balls drew up, and his hips moved against my chin. Pulling him free from my mouth, I pulled my fist up and down on his length as I sucked on the skin of his balls. His hand found the back of my head while he held the wall of the shower.

When I ducked a little more and licked the skin behind his sack into my mouth, he shuddered and hissed, pulling my face deeper. Pre-cum flowed over my hand as I moved faster. I sucked the skin into my mouth, and he yanked me back by my hair.

"Jesus fucking Christ," he said in astonishment before he sucked my tongue into his mouth and pulled my pussy apart before fucking me into the wall. My hands found the sides of his face as he filled me, circling his hips against my clit and pulling another orgasm from me. I clung to his shoulders as I clenched around his hard dick as he roared out his own orgasm.

We stayed there, breathing hard, the water still going and steam rising. My body tingled, every nerve alive, humming with the echo of his touch on my skin. Az was the only thing holding me up. My legs were gelatinous, and I didn't mind it. In his arms, the weight of everything was no longer pressing down on me.

Us—our relationship—we shouldn't make as much sense as we did.

I was a con artist, a liar, running so fast from nothing in particular. He was a predator, all sharp edges and purpose, the kind of man who you'd never want to get on the bad side of. We were jagged, mismatched pieces from two different puzzles. But somehow, when we came together, we fit.

He understood the darkness in me because he carried his own. He didn't flinch from it, didn't judge me for it. Instead, he drew it out, laid it bare, and made me look at it—not with shame, but with the kind of clarity that left me breathless.

And me? I saw the fire in him and wanted to stand close enough to feel its heat without burning alive.

We were chaos and control, light and shadow. I wasn't naive enough to think that made us safe or easy. We weren't. We'd never be easy. But standing there in his arms, my skin still buzzing from his touch, his words still echoing in my ears, I knew one thing for certain: We were perfect for each other, not despite the chaos, but because of it.

I turned my head to look at him, the heavy feeling in my chest overwhelming. His arm tightened around me, as if sensing my gaze, and a small smile tugged at the corner of his mouth.

He was mine. And for the first time in years, I wasn't afraid to be someone's.

It took us a while to untangle ourselves from each other. The lazy kisses and caresses were everything we both needed at that moment. As we dried off, we tied the fluffy towels around our bodies and walked out of the bathroom, leaving our clothes in the shower.

As we walked to the stairs, the clock chimed one 'o'clock. Az looked at me, his eyes full of pride and adoration, and he kissed my lips.

"Happy Christmas," he said, guiding me to the first step so he could look me in the eye.

"Merry Christmas," I replied, running my thumb along his beard. "I love you." I didn't plan them. The words just tumbled out of my mouth. He buried his face in my neck and hugged me tight. He leaned behind me and grabbed something behind me and slipped it into my hand.

The cuff was hammered gold. Sekhmet was on one side and Iris was on the other. Their hands were stretched out, as they held up the most gorgeous piece of lapis lazuli I had ever seen. It was an ode to me and my mother. My fingers traced the Isis as I slipped it on to my wrist. It was a perfect fit. Everything about it was immaculate.

"Azreal."

He smiled at me, really smiled, and I felt tears burning in my eyes.

"Thank you." I tried and failed to stop the tears from coming. Wiping at them quickly, I gave him a watery smile. "You know, if these are the kind of Christmas gifts you're giving out, I think I'm gonna have to stick around. Damn the twelve days."

Az's eyes shined as he grabbed my chin and lifted my chin for a kiss.

"I can make that happen. As long as I get you three hundred and sixty-five days a year," he whispered against my mouth.

"Deal," I whispered back.

THE END

FROM AYLA'S DESK

Well, hi!

Thank you for diving into this dark romance with me! I hope that you were able to feel a little of the Christmas spirit through Eden and Az!

Writing this was an amazing time. I was kicking my feet and cackling and that is always my marker that my readers are going to have a great time.

It's been a full year since I started this journey, and I am so grateful to be here to share my words and imagination with all of y'all.

I spent so much of my life trying to squeeze myself into a box to be like everyone else. Let this be your reminder that your uniqueness is needed and wanted and coveted. It's okay to let it out!

To my ride or dies: I see you and I love you so much. Thank you for speaking that love and kindness into me. I receive it!

To my Shenan ladies: This book wouldn't have happened had y'all not encouraged me to keep pushing. This holiday season I am grateful for the friendship, kindness, and trust we have with one another. You make the journey an amazing one.

To MM: BITCH. You. Already. Know. Forever & Always.

Until the next one, may your cup be ever full and your cum runneth over.

Love,

ABOUT AYLA

Thank you for diving into Ayla Cox's world for a little while.

When Ayla's not on her knees in a fit of passion and lust, she's devouring any book she can get her hands on.
On the off chance that Ayla has time off, you may find her frolicking on a beach or hiding away in a lake cabin, recharging her batteries, both figuratively and literally.
If you love what you've read, give her a follow and leave a few encouraging words.

Sign up for her newsletter at:
https://www.aylacox.com/#newsletter

MORE FROM AYLA

Just a Taste Series

Tempted

Addicted

Insatiable

www.ingramcontent.com/pod-product-compliance
Lightning Source LLC
Chambersburg PA
CBHW021955120726
47992CB00001B/261